"Lissa needs to have something good happen to her. So I think I'll try to get her together with Rory. They're perfect for each other."

Connor snorted. "It's obvious *they* don't think so."

"Look, Connor." My hands were stretched out in front of me, palms up. "You have to understand something about people like Lissa and Rory. They're so used to being pursued by members of the opposite sex that they just wait for people to come to them. They never make any effort. They never notice anyone. They've got to be led together, like in novels."

"You honestly believe that?" Clearly, from his expression, he didn't."

BARBARA COHEN has published several books for children and young adults. She and her husband live in New Jersey. They have three daughters.

LOVERS'
GAMES

LOVERS' GAMES

Barbara Cohen

Pacer BOOKS FOR YOUNG ADULTS

a member of the Putnam Publishing Group

NEW YORK

Published by Pacer Books,
a member of The Putnam Publishing Group
51 Madison Avenue
New York, New York 10010

ISBN: 0-399-21081-4

RL: 6.0

Pacer is a trademark of The Putnam Publishing Group
Reprinted by arrangement with Atheneum Publishers
Printed in the United States of America
First Pacer printing 1984

LOVERS'
GAMES

Chapter One

. . . A hand grasped Mr. Allerton's wrist, and his cousin's voice said urgently in his ear: "Timothy, come quickly to my aunt's dressing room! I must speak to you alone!"

A horrible premonition that the champagne had run out and the ice melted away seized Mr Allerton. But the news, which Henrietta had to impart to him had nothing to do with domestic arrangements. She was clutching in one hand a sheet of writing paper, with part of the wafer that had sealed it still sticking to its edge, and this she dumbly proffered. Mr Allerton took it, and mechanically lifted his quizzing-glass to his eye. "What the deuce—?" he demanded. "Lord, I can't read this scrawl! What is it?"

"Trix!" she uttered, in a strangled voice.

"Well, that settles it," he said giving the letter back to her. "Never been able to make head or tail of her writing! You'd better tell me what it is!"

"Timothy, it's the most terrible thing! She has eloped with Jack Boynton!"

THE MOMENT of Trix's elopement was the very instant selected by Trilby to settle herself in my lap, directly on top of the book I was reading. Trilby was a beautiful tricolor cat, and I loved her. But I was just getting to the romantic part of the story, the part that I would like the best. I put my arm under Trilby's belly, lifted her to the loft floor, and returned to my book.

I was sitting on the loft floor myself, wrapped in an old chenille bedspread we used at the beach. In its former life, our garage had been a barn. Behind the smell of gasoline and oil still lingered faint traces of the rich odors of hay and manure. A narrow ladder led up to the loft, used now to store snow tires, lawn furniture and various other seasonal accoutrements. Other than Trilby and me, no one else had reason, in early October, to scrabble up. The lawn furniture was already put away; the snow tires were not yet needed.

Trilby, a stray, had chosen the loft as a maternity ward. No one knew of her existence but me. I brought her food every day, so she stayed. She was my secret. I had read straight through the novels of Daphne DuMaurier that summer, and when I learned from the note on one of the book jackets that her grandfather George had been a novelist too, I dug out a couple of his musty volumes still owned by the Winter Hill public library. *Trilby* was about a singer caught in the power of a hypnotist named Svengali. My cat was Trilby; I was Svengali. I had her in my power. She would never leave me.

Trilby had found the loft, and I had found Trilby because it was my hiding place too. On an empty Saturday, when she was intent on dragging me off to boutiques and department stores, my mother would look for me first in my room. She might never discover me in the loft. Perhaps I would be safe for a whole afternoon. Perhaps I would be permitted to actually finish my extremely delicious romance.

Up in that loft, perched high above Mother's Cadillac and Aunt Carrie's BMW, I had read the Brontë sisters and Jane Austen, and all their imitators, like Georgette Heyer and Victoria Holt and Mary Stewart. My girl friends mooned over Timothy Hutton and Andy Gibb, or the quarterback of the high school football team. They thought I didn't care. They didn't know I was mooning over Edward Fairfax Rochester and Fitzwilliam Darcy. It was the same thing, really. But I liked my secret lovers better than theirs.

Mine looked just like I wanted them to look. Besides being dazzlingly attractive, their conversation was invariably witty and stimulating. As for Catherine Earnshaw and Elizabeth Bennet, they looked just like me.

Or just the way I wished I looked, or imagined I'd look in a better-ordered world. In real life no boy had glanced at me twice or was ever likely to. And if he did, I wouldn't have known what to do about it.

It wasn't that I was ugly. I just didn't look much like your good old all-American teen-ager is supposed to look. I was very thin, with breasts no bigger than buttons, and I wore my frizzy black hair in a single thick braid down my back. I was almost sixteen and might pass for as much as twelve, from far away in a dim light.

My father thought I was pretty. He told me so at least once a day when he was home. He called me "Duchess," the most incongruous nickname possible for a steel-wool topped stick like me. If ever I was tempted to regard his estimation of my appearance as anything more than the understandable delusion of a fond parent, I had but to look at my cousin Lissa. Next to her, even normally attractive girls faded into the woodwork.

Perhaps Lissa was the real reason I spent so much time up in the loft with Rhett Butler and Heathcliff and Maxim DeWinter. What names. After knowing them, how could anyone love Stan Schneiderman or Willie Travertine? Stan and Willie were two of Lissa's most persistent suitors. She went with them alternate weeks. Occasionally, Iggie Rowson and Rob Palowski were granted a day or two. She didn't really like any of them. She hadn't had a boy friend she really liked since Howie Pridman had moved to Santa Clara, a continent away, and never written her a single letter. Not even a post card.

Howie Pridman was unusual. Most guys, once they caught sight of her, seemed as unable to resist Lissa as Trilby was to resist catnip. Her name was actually Melissa, but everyone called her Lissa, just as my name was actually Amanda Jane, and everyone called me Mandy. Everyone, that is, except my mother. Melissa or Lissa, they suited her equally. As for me, I was never meant to be an Amanda Jane. I was only plain old Mandy.

In my more reasonable moments, I recognized that Lissa had never in her life done me, or anyone else, deliberate harm. But mostly I was too blinded by her light to feel anything much for her but envy. Lissa was so beautiful that sometimes I just stared and stared at her, and other times I could scarcely bear to look at her at all.

People had always drawn in their breath as soon as they laid eyes on her. I first noticed that fact when she was only eight, and she and Aunt Carrie came for a long visit to our big old Victorian house right after her parents' divorce. I hadn't seen a whole lot of Lissa before that.

And then it turned out that Judge Mulvaney was looking for a secretary. Aunt Carrie took the job and just sort of stayed on. Mother had said it would be wonderful for me to have a cousin to grow up with. She and her sister Carrie had always been close, and she said now I would have someone to be a sister to me, too.

It never worked out that way. Not that Lissa and I fought much. We were just sort of indifferent to each other. We didn't care about the same things. And suppose I *had* cared about what Lissa cared about? What would have been the point of that? If I went into competition with Lissa, there'd be only one outcome to that struggle. I'd be left in a heap on the floor, while Lissa and her skatey-eight boyfriends took meticulous care to avoid stepping on my dead body.

I was better off with my nose in a book,

dreaming I was the girl the hero had always de-sired. At least he knew he'd always desired her by the end, if he hadn't quite known it at the beginning

---

. . . "It was all a jest. I was mad—I never meant to come with you!"

"You had to come with me," retorted the Mar-quis. "I won you, and you're mine."

Miss Morland was trembling a little. "But—"

"I have been in love with you for months, and you know it," said the Marquis.

"Oh!" said Miss Morland on the oddest little sob. "I did think sometimes that you were not—indifferent to me, but indeed, indeed this is impossible."

"Is it?" said the Marquis grimly. "We'll see."

It seemed to Miss Morland that he swooped on her. Certainly she had no time to escape. She was nipped into a crushing embrace and kissed so hard and so often that . . .

"Amanda. Amanda Jane." My mother's sweet, breathless voice floated up to me. "Amanda Jane, I know you're up there. You're not anywhere else, so you must be up there."

I gave up. No point in making her really angry by forcing her to climb the ladder. "Yes, Mother, I'm here," I called.

"Come on down now, honey. We have to go shopping."

I pushed my head over the railing surrounding the loft. "I told you this morning, Mother. I'm not going shopping. I don't need anything."

"Yes, you do, Amanda Jane." My mother had lived in New Jersey for twenty-five years, but she still hadn't lost her southern accent. It was deceptive. It made people think she was gentle and easy-going. I guess she's gentle enough, but she's not easy-going. She has a will of iron. That's a characteristic of southern ladies too, but you have to know a few of them really well to catch on. "You can't go to Aunt Carrie's wedding in a pair of patched jeans. You have to buy a dress."

"It's just a small, informal wedding." I echoed the description of the affair I'd heard her use often enough, even though I knew it was less than accurate. "I have a pair of khakis. They're nice. I can iron them. I'll even wear a blouse instead of a T-shirt. I'll even iron the blouse." I was willing to go very far to impress my mother with my docility.

"No, Amanda, that won't do." My mother's voice was firm. "We can't have Peter's family thinking he's marrying into a bunch of hippies. You'll have to wear a dress."

"But Mother," I moaned, "with you and Aunt Carrie and Lissa and all the rest of the females in our family decked out like Vogue models, no one will even notice me. It won't matter what I wear."

"Amanda Jane, you might as well come downtown with me and buy that dress today. Because if you don't buy it today, your father will make you buy it next week, when he comes home. You know how annoyed he gets when he's bothered with things like that."

Yes, I knew. And if he had to lecture me about obeying my mother, he'd call me Amanda Jane instead of Duchess the whole time he was home. He wasn't ever home long. He was a geologist and earned an enormous amount of money because he was so good at finding oil. Occasionally, Mother went with him if his site was near an interesting town or city. I never did. I had to stay home and go to school. It was because Dad traveled so much that it had seemed to everyone a good idea for Aunt Carrie and Cousin Lissa to move in with us permanently. Eight years later, Carrie was marrying Mr. Peter Rasmussen, and now he was going to move in too. His son, Rory, who was away at college and lived with his mother over in Brookville, could be expected to spend an occasional weekend with us also. Well, that was all right. Ours was a very big house. Still, most people these days kind of divide up into smaller and smaller units, while we keep accreting, like a snowball.

It was generally agreed in Winter Hill that the Cobbs were different. It was probably also agreed that Mandy Cobb was the most different of all. But maybe I shouldn't say that. Maybe that's imagining people took more notice of me that was really very likely.

"Goodbye, Trilby," I whispered. "I'll bring you dinner later." I fed her three times a day. She was a nursing mother and needed lots of nourishment. Then I picked up my book and climbed down the ladder. Mother was already behind the wheel of the Cadillac. I opened the door on the passenger's side and sat down next to her. I always felt so conspicuous in the white boat, but Mother loved it and wouldn't get rid of it even though it drank gas like Stanley Schneiderman drank beer.

Once she pulled out of the garage, Mother

braked and blew the horn. The front door of the house slammed and Lissa flew down the porch steps, graceful as a gazelle, and hopped into the back of the car. I turned around and stared at her as Mother nosed her chariot down the drive. Lissa's thick honey-colored shoulder-length hair had fallen neatly back into place without her even touching it. "I thought you had a dress for the wedding already," I said.

"I do," she replied. "I'm coming to help pick out yours."

"I've got Mother," I said. "That's enough. Too many people are just confusing."

"I asked Lissa to come along," my mother said calmly. "Somehow I always make the wrong choice when I shop for you. I really don't know what kids are wearing nowadays."

"I do," I said.

"No, you don't," my mother replied. "But Lissa does."

"I know what they wear," I repeated stubbornly. "They wear jeans and T-shirts, just like me. Look at Lissa. She's wearing jeans and a T-shirt too."

Lissa only smiled. Really, that's all she had to do. Her smile said, "Come on now, Mandy. You know as well as I do that my jeans and my

T-shirt resemble your jeans and your T-shirt about as closely as Princess Di's wedding gown resembled the Little Match Girl's rags." I couldn't argue with Lissa's condescending expression. My jeans were from Sears and I'd bought the T-shirt two summers ago in the Army-Navy store. Lissa's jeans said "Gloria Vanderbilt" on the back pocket, and so did her deep pink T-shirt, on the sleeve. Both garments fitted her so closely they looked as if they'd been painted on her. Lissa didn't believe in leaving too much to the imagination.

"I want you to look smart at the wedding," Mother said. "And I want you to look your age. I don't want to have to be ashamed of you."

"I'm very sorry, Mother," I said through pursed lips. "I'm very sorry if I ever do anything that you have to be ashamed of."

Mother's hand reached out and patted my knee. "Now, Amanda, don't get up on your high horse. You know I'm never ashamed of what you *do*. I'm very proud of what you do. I'm thrilled to death to have a daughter who gets all A's and edits the school newspaper. You're certainly lucky that you inherited your daddy's mind."

"It's too bad I also inherited his looks," I said, "instead of my mama's." I knew that was what she was thinking, so I figured I might as well say it.

"You could be quite attractive, Amanda Jane, if you only chose to be," my mother replied. "Sometimes I just don't know what's the matter with you."

"I'll tell you what the matter is, Mother. I'm skinny, and I have this odd bony face, with these squinty eyes, and my hair's like steel wool. Why should I rig myself out like a horse on a merry-go-round? I've got better things to do than run around looking ridiculous. I'm a very busy person. I have my schoolwork and the newspaper and my books and my friends. Lissa does her things, Mother, and Mandy does her things, and they're different things. It's about time you accepted that." My head swivelled to the back. "Right, Lissa?"

Lissa wasn't listening. She was staring out the window, her hands folded tight in her lap. Her mind was someplace else.

"Don't you want boyfriends?" my mother asked, her tone deceptively mild.

"I have boyfriends," I said, choosing to deliberately misunderstand her. "Stan Schneiderman and Willie Travertine talk to me every day in study hall."

"Because you're Lissa's cousin," my mother replied, her face expressionless. That was a mean thing to say, but it was certainly too true to deny. "You know that isn't what I mean."

"There's Connor Borne," I said. "The yearbook editor. He's always in the publication room the same time I am."

I could almost see her ears perk up. "Oh, yes, Connor Borne. Did you know he's coming to the wedding? His father and Peter are cousins. You see, you really do need a nice dress."

I sighed. I had to straighten this one out before it went any further. The best thing to do was put the blame on her. "Mother, what fibs you make me tell. Connor isn't what you mean either. He's my friend, and he's a boy, that's all."

"Connor isn't anyone's boyfriend," a voice chimed in from the back. Lissa had returned to us. "Connor's not the kind who goes out with girls."

I nodded my agreement. "Who would know better than you, Lissa?"

"Every boy goes out with girls," my mother insisted. "Sooner or later. Every normal boy. And every normal girl goes out with boys. Sooner or later."

I was tired of the conversation. We'd had it too many times before. "Maybe I'm not normal," I suggested. "Leave me alone, Mother. I'm perfectly happy the way I am."

My mother shook her head. She didn't really believe me. And of course it wasn't quite true. "I hoped and prayed that some of Lissa would rub off on you," she said. "But I've given up on that. All I want from you is that you look like a human being at Carrie's wedding and not like a drowned cat."

"Cats look nice," I said. "I'd like to look like a cat. I'd like to look just like Trilby."

"Who's Trilby, for heaven's sake?" Lissa asked.

"Oh, she's a cat living up in the loft," I said. "I don't know where she came from. She's a tri-color and she's beautiful. She has six kittens. They're beautiful too."

"That cat must belong to someone," my mother said. "She'll have to go back."

"I'll keep the kittens," I said.

"Six kittens?" Lissa's brows shot up. "You can't keep six kittens. You'll have to drown at least five of them."

"I won't drown one of them," I retorted. "And I won't let anyone else drown them either. I'll find a way." It had been a mistake to mention them.

Mother shook her head. "Sixteen. Sixteen

and straight A's. But to hear you talk, you'd think you'd never gotten past the fourth grade."

"I'm not sixteen yet," I shot back. "And I wish I still was in the fourth grade. When I was in fourth grade, everybody left me alone."

My mother had pulled the car into the lot behind Grace Crawford's. She and Aunt Carrie bought most of their clothes there, and Lissa bought hers there too when she wanted something particularly classy. I'd never been inside the place before. I broke into a sweat just looking in its elegant windows. By the time we were through the door and into the richly carpeted and chandeliered interior, I felt as if I were as large and as dirty as Beanstalk Jack's giant, sure to soil or rip or knock over something if I dared so much as exhale.

Grace Crawford herself, tall, white-haired and *distingué,* came toward us. Her eyes slid right past me as if I didn't exist. "Why Mary Belle," she said, "what can I do for you today? Or is it lovely Lissa who's looking for something?"

"Surely, Grace, you know my daughter," Mother replied coolly. I'll say this for my mother —she herself might devil me nearly to death, but let someone outside our house so much as faintly imply I was less than perfect and her lovely southern manners turned to ice in a flash. I mean, there was no doubt that my mother loved me. Even I never doubted it. She just didn't know what to do with a daughter like me. Lissa should have been her daughter. Would that have meant I'd have had Aunt Carrie for a mother? That wouldn't have been any better. Or maybe if Lissa had been my mother's daughter, I wouldn't have existed at all. Even in my most depressed moments, I could recognize that as the worst of all possible alternatives.

"She needs a dress for Carrie's wedding," Mother went on. "Something youthful, of course, and smart."

Grace Crawford's eyes focused on me at last. "Don't you think you ought to take her down to Kid's 'N' Things?" she asked. "The O'Hares have some lovely things in there."

I managed a small smile. "That's right, Miss Crawford," I said. "That's where I belong. That's what I told my mother."

"She's sixteen," Mother said through narrowed lips. "She hasn't bought a thing in a kiddie shop in four years." She didn't add that I hadn't bought much of anything anywhere else either.

Poor Grace Crawford. I could see the look of dismay in her eyes as she realized she'd made a mistake. She didn't want to insult my mother. If she added what Mother spent in her shop each year to what Aunt Carrie and Lissa spent, it probably totalled over five thousand dollars. Grace Crawford wasn't going to find too many other customers like the Cobbs and Koerners in Winter Hill. She took my arm. "Come along to the back," she said. "I have just the thing for you, I know."

Of course she didn't, but Mother and Lissa decided to buy it anyway. It was pale blue chiffon in tiers. It looked only a little like a potato sack on me, and Grace Crawford assured us that Carmella was just a miracle worker and wouldn't have any difficulty at all taking it in, and she wouldn't even charge for the alterations, though they were extensive. The dress was marked $99.99, but Grace Crawford said we could have it for $79.99. For $79.99 I could have bought eight hardcover or twenty-four paperback romances, or four old Fred Astaire-Ginger Rogers movies to play on the Betamax. Instead I was stuck with a blue chiffon dress that made me look like an orphan. Though it was brand new, on me it appeared to be a hand-me-down. But I didn't say much. If I had complained, my mother wouldn't have bought it. "You have to like it too," she said. "A girl can't look beautiful unless she believes in her clothes herself. It doesn't matter what other people think."

"It's OK," I said. If I had told her the truth —that it was horrible—we'd have left Grace Crawford's and gone on to Levitsky's Department Store and from there to all the other shops in Winter Hill. And if we hadn't found anything suitable in any of them, we'd have driven to one of the big shopping malls, and then on to another, if need be. My mother and Lissa were perfectly prepared to make a whole day's expedition out of this affair. I just wanted to get it over with.

"Just OK?" Mother asked. "I think it's quite lovely. Don't you, Lissa? It's right, isn't it? It's what girls are wearing, isn't it?"

Lissa glanced at me, and then her eyes fell away. "Half the girls are getting chiffon for the Charity Ball," she said.

"The Charity Ball!" I exclaimed. "That's nearly three months away."

Lissa shrugged. "It's something to talk about."

"You don't think this is perhaps too dressy, then, for an afternoon wedding?" Mother asked, a small frown creasing her otherwise totally unwrinkled forehead.

"For the ball they're getting *long* chiffon," Lissa said. "This is short, so it's fine. It's beautiful. A beautiful dress. I think Mandy looks swell."

Since Lissa was neither stupid nor blind, I realized she was, for some reason or other, as bored with this shopping expedition as I was. Maybe she really didn't care much for shopping unless the figure being dressed was her own. Anyway, my mother said we'd take the thing, and Carmella came in and spent half an hour struggling to make it fit, and Grace Crawford wrote up a charge slip and told Mother the dress would be ready the following Saturday. Carmella pursed her lips together but said nothing. She had her work cut out for her, taking in every seam that dress possessed in a week's time.

"We'll have to go for shoes now," Mother said.

"My white sandals will do," I said.

"In October?" Mother said. She sounded as if I'd suggested attending the wedding barefoot.

"I have a pair of little silver pumps," Lissa said. "I wore them to the prom last spring. They'll fit Mandy. Our feet are about the same size." That was true. Lissa was several inches taller than I was, but she had a very small foot for her height.

"That's awfully nice of you, Lissa," I said. I meant it. Her offer was unexpected, and appreciated because it was going to spare me wasting more time running in and out of shops.

She shrugged. "It's nothing," she murmured.

"Do you need anything, Lissa?" my mother asked. "We outfitted Amanda Jane with such dispatch that we have time for you now."

My heart sank. I was not to escape to the loft after all.

But Lissa said, "No thanks, Aunt Mary. I don't need anything."

I thought something really must be the matter with Lissa. I had never before heard her turn down the opportunity to shop for herself. I felt more in charity with her than I had since we were ten and played paper dolls together. That had been the one thing we'd both liked doing. We had sets and sets of paper dolls, all stored neatly in egg cartons under our beds. Lissa chose their clothes and I made up the stories they lived through. I wondered where those boxes were now. I couldn't remember throwing them out, but somehow it must have happened.

Chapter Two

WE WENT into the Copper Kettle for a good lunch and then we drove home. I climbed back up into the loft and spent the rest of the afternoon engrossed in love stories. I didn't stop until the light in the loft was too dim to read by. I never gave Lissa another thought until I returned to the house to wash up for supper.

We had a powder room on the first floor and two bathrooms on the second, but I liked to use the one on the third floor, which I shared with Lissa. She and I were the only ones who lived at the top of the house. We each had our own bedroom, with a third between us, just for storage. They were big, wonderful old rooms, with lots of eaves and crannies. I wouldn't have traded my bedroom for any one of the plasterboard modern cubicles my friends lived in, even though up there in the attic, I tended to freeze in the winter and roast in the summer.

When I turned the knob of that third floor bathroom, however, I realized the door was locked. "Hurry, Lissa," I called automatically. "I have to wash up for supper too." Lissa would spend four hours a day in the bathroom if you let her. She always had a lot to do in there, between her skin and her hair and her nails and every other part of herself that had to be cleaned and oiled and made up and tended to in a dozen other ways.

"You can wash downstairs," came the muffled reply. The voice that said those words was not the one I expected to hear. I recognized it as Lissa's, but it sounded as if there were a lot more between her and me than just the bathroom door.

"Lissa, what's the matter?" I asked.

"Nothing."

"Yes, something's the matter. I know there is. I can tell from your voice." Her tone was usually calm, light, clear and controlled. She hadn't cried since she was ten, at least so far as I knew. But she was crying now. That's why she sounded so strange to me.

The bathroom door swung open. "The trouble with this house is no one has any privacy," she complained. The sob had disappeared from her voice, to be replaced by annoyance. But her eyes were red and swollen.

"Listen, Lissa, what's the matter? Why have you been crying?" I was so shocked to see her cream and rose complexion soiled by tears that I actually stretched out my hand. "Is there anything I can do?"

"You? What can you do?" She shook her head. "What can anyone do? I don't know what's gotten into me anyway." She brushed past me and walked briskly down the hall to her room.

I followed her. "Lissa, maybe you should tell me." She didn't have any close friends. I mean, she had friends, but no close ones. She was too pretty and too popular for that. Girls hung around her, perhaps hoping to catch some of her aura, or pick up her leftovers, but they were too jealous of her to be really good friends. We certainly weren't good friends either, but she *was* my cousin. "It isn't good to bottle up your feelings," I added, quoting the school nurse's stunning oversimplification of all modern psychological knowledge.

She whirled around then, framed in the open doorway of her bedroom. "You can't help," she said. Her voice was low and furious. "What could you know about the way I feel? You have a mother and a father who live together. You have a mother and a father who love each other." Then she slammed the door.

Slowly I walked back to the bathroom.

Slowly I washed my hands and face. Slowly I dried them. I patted down my hair. And then, still very slowly, I walked down two flights of stairs for dinner.

I sat in the back parlor with my mother and Aunt Carrie while they drank their before-dinner cocktails. I sipped Coke. I didn't say much. They didn't notice. They were too busy talking about the wedding. They didn't even notice that when Lissa came down at last she too was unusually silent. But she had repaired her face. No one could tell from looking at her that a few minutes before it had been puffed and misshapen from her tears.

For so long I had thought of Lissa simply as the most perfect, the most fortunate, the most blessed of girls that now I found myself staring at her in idiotic amazement. She had troubles, like anyone else. I had been too wrapped up in my own dreams and my own worries to notice.

I couldn't be sure what was bothering her. But I had a pretty good idea. I didn't know how to bring it up, though. She might just get mad at me again, the way she had when I had pressed her upstairs earlier. And maybe if she wanted to be left alone, I should leave her alone. But if what was bothering her was what I thought it was, she certainly couldn't talk about it with her mother, or her father, whom she wouldn't see again until Christmas. Maybe I didn't love Lissa, but she'd never done anything to make me hate her. So I decided I had better try to get her to talk about her trouble with me.

It was our job to clear the table and do the dishes. When we were alone in the kitchen, I said to her, "Lissa, I don't blame you for snapping at me, upstairs, before dinner. In your position, I'd have done the same thing. But now, please, listen to me, and try not to get mad."

Without saying a word, she handed me a stack of salad bowls to arrange in the dishwasher.

So I went on. "As a matter of fact, I don't think I'd be as nice about it as you're being, not showing anyone how you really feel."

"How do you know how I really feel?" she snapped.

"I don't. I'm just guessing."

She sighed. "Oh, Mandy, I'm sorry. I'm sorry for yelling at you. But I'm just so jealous of you. So jealous."

I shook my head. I had to laugh a little. "You're jealous of me." It was a statement, not a question. She had made me see that I did have something another person might envy. I hadn't known that before. "That's very funny," I added.

She scraped chicken bones from the plates into the garbage without once looking at me. "I've always been jealous of you," she admitted, "with your storybook mother and father, happily married to each other. Mrs. Halliday said to me, 'Isn't it nice, Lissa, that your mother is marrying Peter. You'll have a father now too.' What an idiot she is."

I nodded. "You already have a perfectly good father." I knew she liked him a lot, even though he lived in Houston and saw her only at Christmas and again in the summer, when she spent a month with him.

"I know it's silly," she explained. "I knew it was silly even when I was small. But I always had this daydream that Mom and Dad would get together again one day. Remember that movie where Hayley Mills played identical twins who didn't even know the other one existed until they met each other at a summer camp, and then they got their parents back together again?"

"Yes, I remember. It was dumb movie, but I loved it."

One by one, she arranged the dirty forks in neat rows in the flatware basket of the dishwasher. "I didn't just love it. I adored it. I went to see it every day while it was playing in town. It was my own fantasy being acted out up there on the screen. Well, you see, with Mom getting married, my dream is over." She glanced in my direction and then back at the forks in her hand, treating each one as carefully as if it were made out of gold. "It can't happen. I have to give it up. And when people say, 'Oh, Lissa, how nice for you. You'll have a daddy now too,' I have to smile and agree and act happy and pretend to be about five years old."

"And no one has noticed. No one has even noticed. Not even your own mother."

"I don't want her to notice," Lissa replied. "She's happy. Why should I spoil that? It's so wonderful for her to be happy."

"My lord, Lissa," I cried, "how can one person be perfectly beautiful like you are, and perfectly good too? You're just like the princesses in the fairy tales." What was I saying? Yet at that moment it seemed to me to be true.

She reached over and put her arm around me, giving me a fleeting hug. "Silly Mandy. I'm so far from good it isn't even funny. You know that better than anyone. But thanks for saying it."

I thought for a moment. "I guess you're

right," I agreed. "You're certainly not very good to Stan Schneiderman, or Willie Travertine or Rob Palowski."

She giggled. "They're just jerks. Who could be nice to them?"

"They're not all jerks," I said. "Willie Travertine isn't a jerk. And Carl Steedman certainly isn't a jerk. He calls you and you hang up on him ten seconds later. Another girl would give her eye teeth to have guys like Carl Steedman or Willie Travertine in love with them."

"Name one." Lissa snorted.

"Maybe me," I replied softly. "You know, you're jealous of me, Lissa. Maybe sometimes I'm jealous of you."

"Don't be, please. You have no reason to be." I blinked my eyes hard, and she hugged me once again. "You know, Mandy, I feel better. It was good to spit it out. It was good to say it to someone."

"Yeah, that's what Mrs. Imfeld says." Mrs. Imfeld was the school nurse.

"Well, she's a bigger jerk than Stan or Willie, but I guess she's right about that much." Lissa looked me straight in the eye for a long moment. "I'm glad I told you, not her," she added quietly. "Thanks, Mandy."

"You're welcome, Lissa."

After that she had to rush because she had a date with Willie. She may have thought he was a jerk, but she didn't mind going out with him, because he had lots of money and was more than willing to spend it. No, Lissa wasn't perfect. But she was a lot nicer than her own cousin had given her credit for being. I felt like an absolute louse. I had been too busy with Rhett Butler and the other dark strangers to notice what was going on right under my nose. But I suppose it isn't totally surprising that I liked Lissa a lot better once I realized she wasn't living in a rose garden any more than I was.

Monday I felt even lousier because when I came into my room after school, there on my bed was a little package wrapped in flowered paper and tied with a flowered ribbon. I opened it to find one of those skinny little books with a colored photograph of the sunset over the ocean on the cover. The kind of book you buy in card and gift shops, it was entitled FRIENDSHIP, and inside were about twenty gooey poems and sayings, each one on a separate page with lots of white space. It was an awful little book, but I almost cried when I read the inscription written on the flyleaf. "It's good to have a friend. A person doesn't really need more than one. Love, Lissa."

Later, when I thanked her, she just said, "Oh, it's nothing." I could see from the way she gave her head a nervous shake that she didn't want to talk about it. So we didn't. Mostly she acted the same as she always had. But sometimes, especially when Peter was over for supper, or wedding plans were being discussed, which was pretty much most of the time, I could see her eyes glaze over, and I had the feeling that although her body was still in the room, her mind had gone off somewhere on its own. Wherever that place was, it wasn't terribly pleasant. Then I wished there was something I could do for her, really do for her. But I couldn't think what. She was not the kind of person who appeared to need anything—except what was beyond my power, or anyone's, to give her.

The week before the wedding I didn't see much of her. She was going out with one guy or another not just on weekends, but on week nights too. And I was at school every evening until seven or eight o'clock, getting out the paper. Between the caterer and the florist, our house was in such an uproar that Lissa and I were both anxious to stay out of the way.

I sat with some of the other members of the newspaper staff, eating sandwiches while we pored over rewrites, galleys and dummies, blotting up with copy paper the mayonnaise and mustard that dripped onto the sheets in front of us. "Where's page two of the football story?" the sports editor would scream, while the assistant feature editor sat at the typewriter hastily inventing a joke to fill a hole on her page. The confusion was mind-splitting. I loved it.

The yearbook kids were in the publication room the same time we were, just adding to the chaos. They had a deadline too that week. I stood at a work table dummying up the editorial page, when Connor Borne came by and reached for my paste pot. He was a senior, and I was only a junior, but I'd known him all my life.

"Hey, Connor, what do you think you're doing?" I scolded.

"I'm only borrowing it for a second, Mandy," he apologized. "I'll bring it right back. My pot's empty, and I'm just going to dump a little of yours into it."

"Get some from one of your own staff." He had his hand on top of my pot, and I put my hand on top of his.

"Oh, come on, kiddo, what difference does it make?" he wheedled. "It's all Winter Hill High School paste."

"The thing I don't understand," I complained, "is why you guys have to be here the very same week we are. I mean, you have a deadline once a year, we have one once a month. Why couldn't you have done all this stuff last week, when we weren't around? Now we're fighting over worktables and scissors and paste. It's silly."

"Well, it may seem silly to you, but unfortunately I don't think there's anything we can do about it." Connor wasn't annoyed with me. He never was. Connor always spoke to me with the voice of sweet reason. He was tall and skinny and sort of ascetic looking, with thick glasses, a long nose and a face covered with acne pimples. At the moment his poor sunken cheeks looked even more like the moon's surface than usual because he'd begun growing a beard. But so far as I knew, he'd never in his life lost his temper. He was the ideal editor of a student publication. I was not.

"You see," he continued in his best pedagogical style, "we don't set our own deadlines. The company that prints the yearbook tells us when we have to have each section done if we're to receive the books before school is out. You can understand that. They print yearbooks for thousands of schools. If everyone sent the stuff in whenever they felt like it, it would all come in

April and May and they'd have some mess on their hands down there in that printing plant in Texas. . . ."

I think he might have gone on for an hour explaining to me the exact process by which the yearbook was put together if I hadn't grunted with impatience. "If you know when your deadlines are from the beginning of the year, why do you rush to meet them at the last minute?" I asked. "I mean it's different for us. We have to do everything at the last minute because we're supposed to be a *news*paper. That means we should print the most recent stuff we can."

His face broke into a grin. He had a lovely grin. When he smiled a person more or less forgot how homely he was. "Oh, come on, kiddo. What's a deadline but something you have to rush to meet? Whoever heard of a bunch of kids getting themselves together to do things two weeks or even one week before a deadline? Whoever heard of *anyone* doing that?"

Well, that was the truth. I had to grin back at him and capitulate. "Just don't use all the paste. I still need it. And bring the pot right back."

"Yes, Mother." Still smiling, he turned away and walked back to what was supposed to be his end of the room.

Suddenly I remembered something. I hurried after him. "Connor, Connor," I whispered, tapping him on the shoulder.

He turned. "Mandy, I'm sorry, but five seconds with the paste pot is simply not enough. Try to give me ten."

I ignored his remark, which wasn't very funny anyway. "Connor, you're going to the wedding Saturday, aren't you?" I queried.

"Yeah, sure," he said. "Peter is my father's first cousin. Mom and Dad said your folks were nice enough to invite me, so I have to go. I guess they're kind of flattered we were all asked. My dad's father and Peter's may be brothers, but they're not exactly in the same class."

I noted the irony in his tone. "You don't sound as if you're exactly looking forward to the whole business," I said.

"I'm not," he agreed. "Weddings are dumb. I mean, they're not dumb for the couple getting married, but I think they're dumb for everyone else. Getting married is a private thing between two people. Why do they have to drag in the whole immediate world?"

"Maybe so everyone else will know it happened," I suggested. "Maybe so that neither of them will be able to weasel out of it too easily later on."

"Ah, Mandy, you're a cynic." Connor

laughed. "Actually, I'll tell you the real reason I hate to go to weddings. Fortunately, I haven't been slapped with too many. As a matter of fact, I think this is only the second one, and at the last one, I was only eight and thought it was fine. . . ."

"All right already, Connor. Tell me the real reason."

He lowered his voice to a whisper. "It's the suit. Every time I put on a suit I get the most awful case of crotch rot. You wouldn't believe it."

I giggled. "Your suit's too small?"

"It fits all right, I guess. It's psychological. I'm allergic to suits."

"The way I am to dresses," I sympathized. "Listen, wait 'til you see me at the wedding. I'm going to look like a bag lady. So don't laugh, and stay close to me, so I have someone to talk to. Otherwise I may turn into a werewolf and eat up all the guests instead of the buffet."

"Will the food be good?"

"Fantastic," I assured him. Connor ate constantly. I had never seen him without at least a chocolate bar or a bag of potato chips in his hand. Yet he never gained any weight, at least not so that it showed. He just got taller and taller. He needed to eat a lot so that his brain would have enough energy to send the proper messages the enormous distances to his hands and feet.

"OK," Connor agreed. "If you stick close to the buffet table, I'll stick close to you. We'll comfort each other."

Chapter Three

CONNOR and I really did more or less stick together the day of the wedding. Not during the ceremony, though. For that, the bride's relatives were arranged on one side of the room and the groom's relatives on the other. The doors between our front and back parlors had been thrown open. There was plenty of space for everyone to sit on metal folding chairs Mother had borrowed from Mr. Gretz at the funeral home.

First, Judge Mulvaney walked down the aisle between the rows of seats. He wasn't wearing his black robe, but he projected infinite dignity anyway, with his white hair and craggy face. When he reached the bow window, filled with palms and chrysanthemums, he turned around and faced the crowd.

Next came Peter, looking extremely handsome in a dark gray suit. But I didn't spend much time looking at Peter. I was too busy staring at his son Rory, who was walking down the aisle with him. I think my mouth hung open as I gazed at him. I hadn't seen him in at least five years. I'd forgotten what he looked like. It wouldn't have mattered if I had remembered. Between thirteen and eighteen guys change an awful lot. But it seemed to me that Rory had changed even more than most.

Whatever he'd looked like before, that day Rory Ramussen was right out of a romantic novel —any romantic novel. He looked just like Maxim DeWinter or Fitzwilliam Darcy must have looked when they were eighteen. Like his father, he also wore a dark gray suit, in a narrow cut that showed off his modified Mr. America build. It was October, but his skin was still tanned and his curling hair was streaked with gold. His jaw was strong, his mouth full, his nose classical, and his brown eyes large, bright and warm. I couldn't believe a guy could be that handsome and live.

When Peter and Rory reached the bow window, they stood sideways, to the left of the judge. Miss Carscadden was playing "Liebestraum" on the piano when Lissa walked through the double doors. She looked like a Renoir painting in a dress of thin cream-colored cotton. She carried pink roses and smiled as if this was the happiest day of her life. I admired her guts.

Then Miss Carscadden switched to the "Wedding March" from *Lohengrin,* and down the aisle, on my father's arm, came Aunt Carrie. The joy that shone in her eyes dazzled me like sunlight. It was matched by the glow emanating from Peter as he walked toward her to replace my father's arm with his own. Suddenly, tears filled my eyes and an unreasoning sense of happiness surged up inside of me. I knew that I was glad to be at this wedding. For the moment I totally forgot about my frightfully bright blue orphan's dress. For a moment I totally forgot about *me.*

But not for long. The brief ceremony was over, Peter and Aunt Carrie were hurrying back down the aisle, to the strains of Mendelssohn this time, Peter clutching Aunt Carrie's arm as if he were afraid she might float away if he let her go.

Everyone stood up. I had to stand up too. My mother, next to me, tugged at the waist of my dress as if somehow doing that would make it fit better. "This dress was a mistake," I muttered.

"You look lovely, dear," my mother replied. "Blue becomes you. It goes with your eyes." She had said those exact words several times in the past week.

"No one over three wears this shade," I snapped.

Now she was annoyed. "I asked you if you liked it when we were in the store. Why did you let me buy it if you didn't like it?"

"Because I didn't . . ."

But I never finished. Mrs. Delaney tapped her on the shoulder. "Congratulations, Mary Belle," she gushed. "I never saw a prettier wedding. I know how much you had to do with the arrangements. It's all just lovely."

Mother was swept away in flurry of hostessing. I cursed myself for lacking Lissa's self-control. I could have kept my mouth shut about the dress, at least for now, and not spoiled my mother's day. But as I glanced in her direction and saw her chatting happily to six different people at once, she didn't really look like a person whose day had been spoiled. I may not have been the daughter of her dreams, but she wasn't the sort of person to brood about that.

Waiters appeared to take away some of the chairs and set up tables. The guests were spilling out into the hall and onto the porch, where Peter and Aunt Carrie stood receiving congratulations. I headed toward the dining room. Sure enough, there I found Connor, staring steadily at the elaborately laden table upon which the caterer was putting the finishing touches. He knew that he dared not be the first one to fill a plate, but I could see that he restrained himself with difficulty. "Hi, Connor," I said. "I've come to distract you."

"Thank goodness," he said. "The wedding itself didn't turn out to be half bad, but I can't handle this waiting around."

"Come out on the porch," I suggested. "They're passing hors d'oeuvres now, to go with drinks. We have to get through them before we can eat the main food."

"Well, hors d'oeuvres are better than nothing." Connor led the way, and I followed him. The porch was jammed, but plenty of waiters circulated with trays of little frankfurters wrapped in dough and Swedish meat balls and tiny bits of fried chicken. Connor swallowed a dozen in rapid succession and turned back into a human being.

"I thought you might have shaved for the occasion," I said.

"Listen, Mandy, this beard is going to be gorgeous once it comes in," he insisted. "I wouldn't do anything at this stage to jeopardize it." Poor Connor. If there was anyone who looked more out of place that day among all of the beautiful people than me, it was he.

The most beautiful person of all, Rory, was standing next to the bar that had been set up on one side of the porch. He was sipping a glass of Perrier water or club soda and staring out in front of him. I couldn't believe he was all by himself, instead of surrounded by a crowd of smitten teen-aged girls. But then I realized there was no crowd of teen-aged girls present. Lissa and Connor's sister and I were the only ones. Surely Rory's charms did not go unnoticed by older women, but maybe they were too embarrassed to make that fact obvious.

"Let's go over and talk to your cousin Rory," I said. "He's all alone."

"I can live without my cousin Rory," Connor said. "But I suppose at weddings you have to be nice to everyone, like on Christmas."

"You're just jealous," I said.

"Of what?" He sounded genuinely surprised.

"You mean you haven't noticed what he looks like?" Now I was surprised.

"I'm not a girl. Maybe that's why. Nor gay," he added briskly.

I laughed. "Well, that's one difference between men and women for sure," I said. "Women always notice whether another woman is pretty or not. They're always making that kind of judgement."

"I never thought I'd hear such a sexist remark from Amanda Cobb, girl editor," Connor teased.

I considered that for a moment. "I suppose it is a sexist remark," I agreed. "But it's true." I turned and headed through the crowd toward Rory. I wasn't sure whether or not Connor would accompany me, but he followed right on my heels.

Rory saw us coming. "Hi, Connor," he said as we approached. His glance flicked over me without recognition, and without interest, either.

"Don't you remember Mandy?" Connor asked. "She's Carrie's niece."

Still no sign of recognition lit his eyes, but he smiled pleasantly. "Oh, yes. Hi, Mandy. It's been a long time."

"Yeah," I agreed. "The Y day camp probably. We've both changed."

"Oh, now I remember." He seized my hand and shook it. "Boy, my nose never stopped running those summers I went to the Y camp. I had this constantly running nose. It was awful. I must have been allergic to some kind of grass they had up there." He didn't really look like Maxim de Winter. He was too American for that. He looked more like Christopher Reeve. "Did you have a similar problem?" he queried.

"No, I don't think so." I couldn't imagine what I was supposed to say next. Fortunately, Connor stepped into the breach. "How's Yale, old man?"

I had known he was a freshman at Yale. Peter bragged of it often enough. It meant Rory was smart as well as handsome. "OK, I guess," Rory replied. Then he grinned. "As a matter of fact, it's good. It's very good. I feel really privileged to be there. I'm mixing with a really high-level bunch of guys."

"A high-level bunch of guys, huh?" Connor seemed to be turning the phrase over on his tongue and deciding he didn't much like the taste. Nevertheless he added, "I'm applying." I couldn't imagine anyone who looked less like a Yale man than Connor.

"Oh really?" An expression of slight surprise flickered in Rory's eyes and then was rapidly banished. "Lots of good luck. What's your class rank?"

Connor's voice was cool. "Number two."

Rory nodded. "And your SAT's?"

"1520," Connor replied lightly.

At this Rory couldn't quite suppress a look of respectful amazement. "I guess you'll get in," he said, "if you have any activities."

"I'm yearbook editor," Connor said. "And starting center on the basketball team."

Then I knew he was lying. Connor was a year ahead of me; I knew nothing about his class rank or his SAT scores. But I did know for sure that Billy Oates was the starting center on the basketball team. Connor Borne wasn't on the team at all. He was tall, all right, but about as well coordinated as a scarecrow.

"Look me up when you get there," Rory said.

"I'm just considering Yale," Connor returned. "I may not actually *go* there. I think I might prefer Harvard or Princeton. Or even MIT, if I decide I want to take up engineering."

"Yale's the best," Rory said. His face was concerned and serious. "Even if you want to be an engineer, come to Yale. Get a good, strong liberal arts background, and then go to graduate school. You're too young to make a decision now that will limit you for the rest of your life." I hardly heard what he said. I was too busy watching the white teeth that gleamed behind his perfect lips as he spoke.

"I can get a good liberal arts education at Harvard or Princeton, certainly," Connor said. "Yale seems—well, it seems a bit provincial to me."

"No, no," Rory insisted, growing quite excited. "Princeton is provincial, not Yale. And there's too much pressure at Harvard. It's like a steam bath. They just grind, grind, grind there. You want to get the best education you can, but at the same time, you want to have a little fun." I wondered if Rory really did have fun. He was entirely pleasant, but he didn't smile much, or make jokes.

Connor nodded and stroked the wisps of hair on his chin. "I'll take what you're saying under advisement. I'll certainly consider it."

Connor was teasing Rory, and Rory didn't even know it. I didn't think Connor was being very nice. "I will too," I said.

"You?" Rory's eyebrows shot up. "Little Mandy, you've got a long way to go before you have to worry about college." He laughed.

So much for the blue chiffon dress. "I'm sixteen," I said stiffly. No one would call me a liar for two months.

He smiled benignly. "Sorry, honey," he said.

I would have punched him, but I didn't want to spoil that beautiful mouth. I turned away and gazed across the porch. Lissa's arm was caught in the viselike grasp of Dr. Bellinghame, who must have weighed three hundred pounds. He was talking to her intently, but her eyes had wandered toward us. I waved eagerly. She murmured something, managed to pull herself out of Dr. Bellinghame's monstrous fist and push her way through the crowd to us.

"Hi, Lissa," Connor greeted her. "Congratulations. That's what I'm supposed to say, isn't it? You are supposed to congratulate the bride's daughter, aren't you?"

"Are you?" Lissa asked. "Did you congratulate Rory?"

"No, I forgot." Obediently, Connor's head swiveled in the opposite direction. "Congratulations, Rory."

"Yes. Thanks." Like Lissa, Rory was managing to maintain a moderately cheerful demeanor, but he didn't seem any more pleased with the match than she was. Perhaps beneath his phlegmatic facade, he had harbored the same crazy dreams as she. After all, to look at her, you'd never have imagined her to be so fanciful.

"Hey, we're related now!" Connor exclaimed.

"We are?" Lissa responded coolly.

"Yeah, we're step-cousins. And you and Rory—now you're brother and sister." For a clever boy Connor was being awfully dense.

"Step-brother and step-sister," Lissa enunciated carefully.

"Which is really no relation at all," Rory explained, his face unsmiling. "No blood relation. No other kind really matters."

"It doesn't?" I could understand Rory's feelings, but I didn't agree with what he was saying. "No one could be more like brother and sister than Aunt Carrie and my father, and they're not blood relations. They're in-laws. It's the way you feel that matters."

"Well, for them it's been so many years—" Lissa began.

"You agree with him?" I interrupted sharply.

"Well, I agree with you too, of course," Lissa said in a conciliatory tone. "I mean about my mother and your father. But real relatives. . . ."

Connor, as if to make amends for his obtuseness, changed sides. "Well, I know what Lissa is saying. Real brothers and sisters can't get married."

"Yes, that's true," Rory nodded. "That would be incest." There wasn't the faintest trace of irony in his voice.

As there most definitely was in Connor's. "Whereas you two, if you wanted to, could certainly get married. There'd be nothing to stop you."

"Nothing to make us do it, either," Lissa commented.

Rory nodded his agreement. "It would look terrible."

"Actually," I said, suddenly struck by an idea, "it would *look* wonderful. You'd make a handsome couple." A very handsome couple, just like on TV.

The direction of the conversation was clearly troubling Rory, but his manners, like his looks, were perfect. "I see my Aunt Ernestine over there," he said politely. "I really have to say hello to her. Please excuse me."

"Certainly," Lissa replied. She smiled, and then when he was gone, she sighed. I wasn't sure what the sigh meant.

"You never told me he was so gorgeous," I scolded.

"That's because I never noticed," Lissa said.

"Oh, come on, Lissa," I said. "You have to be kidding."

"Actually, I've been with him on only a couple of different occasions," she explained. "I wasn't much in the mood at the time for noticing guys. He's all right, I guess."

"Just all right?" I shook my head. "Cripes, Lissa, he makes Robert Redford look like Pinocchio. I mean, who do you think *is* good looking, if not Rory?"

"Oh, I don't know," she said. "If you think he's so cute, why don't you go after him yourself?"

"Me?" I laughed. "Come off it, Lissa. A guy like him wouldn't give a girl like me a second glance."

"Lissa, tell Mandy to shut up." That was Connor.

I shook my finger in his face. "Be serious, Connor. You know I look like Little Orphan Annie."

Lissa regarded me thoughtfully. "The dress isn't right," she agreed. "I'd feel guilty enough about that even if you hadn't been so nice to me the day we bought it. Well, I'll make it up to you. There is a way for you to dress that would bring out the best in you. We just have to find it."

My mother and her mother weren't enough. Now she was going to go to work on me too. "I have my books and my cats and my newspaper," I said. "I don't want to be bothered with all that other stuff. That stuff's for you, not me."

Lissa laughed. "That's what you say. You

don't mean it. If you meant it, you wouldn't have noticed what Rory looks like."

"This is a dumb conversation," Connor interjected, his foot tapping impatiently. "I can't stand it. I'm going to get something to eat. They must have opened up the buffet table by now."

"I'm sure they have," Lissa assured him.

A figure appeared at the window behind us. Through the screen I could see that it was my mother. "Lissa," she called, "we've been looking all over for you. The photographer wants to get some pictures on the stairs. You'd better come in now."

"Sorry, Aunt Mary," Lissa replied. "I'm coming." She hurried away from us and a few moments later, when Connor and I entered the front hall, we saw her standing on the landing, holding her nosegay of rosebuds. She was next to the wall, and her mother was next to her, and Peter was next to her, and Rory was next to him. They were all smiling. They were all gorgeous. They looked like one of those perfect families in *Good Housekeeping*.

Connor and I filled our plates in the dining room. Actually, Connor filled his plate. I wasn't very hungry. I led him through the swinging doors into the breakfast room. The table was piled high with the caterer's back-up supplies, but I cleared a space big enough for the two of us, and we sat down. After shooting us one dirty look, the caterer ignored us.

"Your Cousin Rory is an interesting person," I said.

"Interesting?" Connor shot back. "He's dumb."

"Listen, Connor, you can't get into Yale and be dumb."

"Oh, he isn't really dumb. Not dumb in the brain," Connor tried to explain. "He's just not very sharp."

"You mean he has no humor," I pointed out. "He takes himself very, very seriously."

"Yes, that's right," Connor said. "That's what I mean."

"But he's nice," I said.

"Nice enough, I guess," Connor mumbled, his mouth full.

"Very nice and smart and handsome. It won't make any difference to Lissa if he doesn't have a sense of humor. She doesn't have much of one either."

Connor actually put his fork down long enough to look me in the eye. "What is it that you have in mind, Amanda Cobb? What deviltry are you contemplating now?"

"I'm not the devil," I retorted. "You are.

Imagine feeding poor innocent Rory all that business about the basketball team. What about the rest of that stuff? I suppose it wasn't true either."

"I'm not second in the class," Connor admitted. "I'm ninth."

"Well, that's not too bad," I allowed. "As long as you were lying, why didn't you go all the way and say you were first?"

"I didn't want to stretch possibility too far," Connor explained kindly.

"And your SAT's?"

Connor murmured something at about the same time that he was stuffing his mouth with a forkful of potato salad.

"What did you say?" I asked.

"That part was true." His eyes were fixed on his plate.

"Hmm," I commented. "So maybe you will get into Yale."

"Not likely, but not impossible," he said. "Only I'm not applying. I want a small school. Wesleyan or Williams or Amherst. Some place like that. If we can come up with the money. Otherwise it's good old Rutgers for me. Which is OK. You can get a perfectly good education there if you want one."

"You're not a snob," I said.

"I can't afford to be," he said.

"Do you think Rory's a snob?" My question was rhetorical. I answered it myself. "No, he isn't. But if he were, that wouldn't matter either, because Lissa is, sometimes."

Again Connor's fork paused in midair, and he turned his face toward mine. "I ask you once more, and for the last time, what is it that you're talking about?"

"I want to do something nice for Lissa," I replied calmly. "She needs to have something good happen to her. So I think I'll try to get her together with Rory. They're perfect for each other."

Connor snorted. "It's obvious *they* don't think so."

"Look, Connor." My hands were stretched out in front of me, palms up. "You have to understand something about people like Lissa and Rory. They're so used to being pursued by members of the opposite sex that they just wait for people to come to them. They never make any effort. They never notice anyone. They've got to be led together, like in novels."

"You honestly believe that?" Clearly, from his expression, he didn't.

"Yes, I do," I said. I wanted him to understand that I was totally sincere. "They're so used to fending off the attacking hordes that it will be a relief for them to be with each other. It will be a delight. With each other, they'll be able to relax and just be themselves."

"Well, why haven't they noticed that?" Connor asked.

Actually, it was a reasonable question. But I had the answer. "Because, you see, they're prejudiced against each other, on account of this wedding. Neither of them likes it very much. You can't blame them. Rory's attached to his mother, just the way Lissa is to her father. I mean, they'll get used to the marriage in time, because they're both nice and I'm sure Rory wants his father to be happy just as I know Lissa wants her mother to be happy. But right now—"

"Yeah," Connor interrupted. "I get you. Right now it's like a new sore. Or like opening up an old one—the divorces they had to live through. I guess we're lucky we never had to handle all that junk."

"Not so far, anyway," I said. "In this day and age you never know. Though," I added very quickly, "things seem absolutely fine between my folks."

"Yeah," Connor said. "With mine too. But

if they weren't, maybe we wouldn't notice. Or maybe we'd notice and sort of pretend we didn't. Hide the truth from ourselves."

I nodded. "That's what Lissa told me once. She said her mother and father fought and fought, and really it was better in lots of ways after they were divorced. But while it was going on, if friends told her their parents were divorcing, she always thought to herself, 'Oh, nothing like that will ever happen to me.' And then it did, and she was totally surprised and hurt and angry, even though she knew all about the fighting."

"It certainly hasn't blighted her life," Connor commented. "It seems to me that she's the most popular girl in the school."

"Well, in a way that's true," I admitted. "But she doesn't really care about any of those guys she goes out with. She hasn't really liked anyone since Howie Pridman. She likes the ones who aren't all over her, the ones who are a little hard to get. That's why I think underneath she really likes Rory. He's not a pushover for her."

"On the contrary," Connor replied drily. "He seems totally indifferent—if not actively hostile."

"Well, we're going to fix them up," I announced firmly.

He drew back. "We? We? Leave me out of this, Amanda Cobb."

"It'll take two of us." I smiled. "Come on, Connor. It'll be fun. That's the real reason to do it—for fun."

"Forget it. It's impossible. It can't be done. I know my cousin Rory. He has all the emotion of a clam. There's nothing you or I can do to move him."

"How much you want to bet?"

He sat forward again. "Bet? Do you mean a real bet?" His brows lifted and his eyes held a challenge.

I hadn't. I had merely been using a figure of speech. But I picked up Connor's gauntlet immediately. "Yes. I mean a real bet. I don't fool around. But if we bet, you've got to help me. If we don't get them together, I lose and you win. But still, you have to promise to act as if it were the other way around."

"Yes," he agreed. "I'll do whatever you tell me to do, and I'll do it wholeheartedly. I don't mind, because I know it's impossible for you to win this bet. Actually, there's nothing in the world I like more than betting on a sure thing."

He smiled, a secret, satisfied smile. I had known Connor Borne a long time. Since before the Y day camp. Since nursery school, actually. And I knew from that smile that he was up to something. But I didn't care. He had promised to help me. That's what mattered. If he made a promise, he'd keep it. He was the dependable, trustworthy type. Or so I had always assumed.

"What's the bet going to be?" I asked. "What are we betting? I mean what do I have that you want?"

He laughed, almost wickedly. For a moment, he didn't sound like dependable, trustworthy Connor at all. "We'll get to that," he said. "But before we settle on how much, we have to decide how long."

"What do you mean?"

"We can drag this thing on forever," he explained. "We have to decide when we'll have tried long enough and hard enough. And we have to have some kind of objective standard for winning or losing. You can't just say we have to get them to like each other. They have to do or not do something that will *show* whether or not they like each other."

I nodded. I understood what he was saying, and he was right. For a moment, we were silent, thinking. The only sound was Connor's chewing. Then he suddenly cried out, "I've got it! I've got it! He has to ask her to the Charity Ball, and she has to say yes. That will be the outward sign. If he asks her to the ball, and she goes with him, you win. If he doesn't ask her, or if he asks her and she says no, then I win."

"What if she asks him?" I suggested.

"If he says yes, that's OK too," Connor agreed magnanimously. "I'm no MCP."

"No, of course not."

"Cut the sarcasm, kiddo. We've got to co-operate. We've got to work together."

"And awfully fast too," I pointed out. "The only time between now and the Charity Ball that Rory is likely to be home is Thanksgiving."

"Oh, come on, Mandy!" Connor exclaimed. "You can do better than that. New Haven isn't so far away. With a little effort you can persuade him to wend his way home every other weekend. Maybe you can even send Lissa up there now and then. A mind as devious as yours should have no trouble thinking up perfectly plausible excuses."

Maybe I was not above some judicious manipulation in a good cause, but I was suddenly suspicious of what was going on in *his* brain. "Listen," I said, "what are we betting? What's the prize? We still haven't decided."

"That," he retorted, "is for me to know and you to find out!"

"What kind of nonsense is that?" I cried. "You think I'm going to let you turn the prize into whatever you want? If I win, you'll say the bet was for five cents, and if I lose, you'll say it was for five hundred dollars."

"Ah, Mandy," he sighed. "You know me better than that. You know I'm an honest man. It would go against my entire character to cheat an old and valued friend like you."

"Oh, yeah?" I laughed shortly. "You're up to something, Connor Borne. I wish I knew what it was. . . ." I had always thought him a Boy Scout, but I'd certainly never put him to the test. And I was just beginning to recognize a gleam in his eye I'd never noticed before.

"It's not worse than what you're up to," he said, pushing his plate away from him at last. "As you said, we're both trying to alleviate the boredom of high school, which has to be the most boring time of a person's existence."

"I don't find it boring," I snapped. "I have plenty to do." I entered upon my usual refrain. "I have my books and the newspaper and. . . ."

"But what about real life, Mandy?" he asked. "What about real life? That's what we're short on at Winter Hill High. That's what we're missing. That's why we have to liven up our days."

"You're crazy, Connor," I told him. "I'm not going to bet with you because you'll cheat me."

He shook his head. "I'll write the bet down today, and I'll put it in a sealed envelope and mail it to Miss Dreyfuss." Miss Dreyfuss was my English teacher and Connor's yearbook adviser. "She can hold it for us. When we know who's won, then we'll open the envelope. You'll be able to tell from the postmark that the prize was established well before we knew who the winner was. That way you can be sure that whatever you get if you win will be worthwhile. I wouldn't make a bet for something I didn't want—something I didn't value."

"But how do I know it'll be something *I* value?" I protested. "It could be . . . it could be . . . a pair of purple jockey shorts."

He shook his head, and suddenly his voice lost its levity. The amusement I'd discovered lurking in his eyes was gone. "I hope with all my heart that by the time that envelope is opened you will want the prize as much as I do. I will do everything in my power to see to it that that happens. I promise you that."

I was somewhat taken aback by the seriousness of his tone. I was amused and intrigued too.

After all, what he was suggesting was rather like the toy at the bottom of a box of Crackerjack. When we were kids we always bought the Crackerjack mainly for the prize, even though we never knew in advance what it was going to be. "All right," I said. "I agree."

"Good." He held out his hand. "Let's shake on it."

I extended mine. He seized it and squeezed it, hard. "It's a bet," he said.

"Yes," I agreed. "It's a bet."

Chapter Four

 IN MISS DREYFUSS'S English class we started reading Shakespeare's comedy *Much Ado About Nothing* out loud. Steve Ellery was Claudio and Bruno Kruczek was Benedick. They were both terrible, so I put my fingers over my ears and read the lines myself.

CLAUDIO: Benedick, didst thou note the daughter of Signior Leonato?

BENEDICK: I noted her not, but I looked on her.

CLAUDIO: Is she not a modest young lady?

BENEDICK: Why, i'faith, methinks she's too low for a high praise, too brown for a fair praise, and too little for a great praise . . .

CLAUDIO: Thou thinkest I am in sport. I pray thee tell me truly how thou likest her.

BENEDICK: Would you buy her, that you inquire after her?

CLAUDIO: Can the world buy such a jewel?

BENEDICK: *Yea, and a case to put it into . . .*
CLAUDIO: *In mine eye, she is the sweetest lady that ever I looked on.*
BENEDICK: *I can see yet without spectacles, and I see no such matter: there's her cousin, an she were not possessed with a fury, exceeds her as much in beauty as the first of May doth the last of December. . . .*

———————

Of course, I was now in love with Benedick. It was nice not to have to wait until late at night or Saturdays to have a hero from a book to dream about. Something had changed, though, in my dreams. No longer did my hero have some vaguely imagined face. He looked exactly like Rory Ramussen.

I felt wonderfully noble as I pursued my plan to bring Lissa and Rory together. I was crazy about Rory myself, yet here I was, unselfishly presenting him to Lissa. However, I knew perfectly well it really wasn't much of a sacrifice. Rory was about as likely to fall for me as he was to fall for a monkey in the zoo, so I might as well do a good deed and gently shove him and Lissa in each other's direction.

———————

Much Ado About Nothing gave me an idea about how to get started. It was lucky we were reading it. Otherwise I might have floundered around for days trying to think something up, and there wasn't any time to lose.

I invited Connor to come up to the loft to visit the kittens and talk about our plans. The weather was turning colder. I knew this was one of my last afternoons in the loft. I wasn't sure if Trilby would spend the winter there or move her kittens some other place. But I hoped it might be warm enough up there for cats, if not for human beings. As long as they stayed, I'd feed them. But I knew that when spring came, if they were still there, I'd have to find the money to have Trilby spayed, and the female kittens spayed too, or else I'd soon have more cats on my hands than the loft could shelter or I could afford to feed.

"You should be flattered," I said to Connor, offering him the littlest kitten to pet. "You're the only person I've ever allowed up here."

He stroked the baby gingerly for about half a second and then withdrew his hand. "I am, I am," he assured me. "But I'd like it just as well without the cats. Better, actually," he added under his breath.

"What did you say?" I asked, to make sure.

"Better, actually," he repeated, lifting his head and looking at me directly.

"You're not a cat person?" I felt absurdly disappointed.

"I don't hate them. I just don't love them. I love people better. Some people."

"Cats have many lovely qualities," I informed him as I knelt to pick up the kitten. "They are very independent and will never humble themselves before you, like certain dogs, but they are nevertheless superior creatures to have around." I plopped down on the old bed spread and patted the place beside me. Connor lowered himself into a sitting position, twisting his long legs in front of him like a pair of pretzels. I delivered myself of a brief lecture on the personal habits of the genus feline.

After I'd droned on for about five minutes I realized that Connor had stretched himself all the way out on the spread and closed his eyes. I tickled him under the ribs. He sat up in an instant, and his arm went around me. His face was so close to mine I could see each of the peppery red hairs that now fringed his cheeks.

I wasn't accustomed to a boy so near me, even if it was only Connor. I pulled away from his arm. "OK," I said, slightly out of breath,

"I'm done with my lecture. Now I'll tell you my plan."

"What plan?" His voice was low; he seemed to have forgotten why we were there.

"My plan. My plan about Rory and Lissa."

"Oh, yeah." He moved himself over several inches, well away from both me and the kitten.

"I got my plan out of *Much Ado About Nothing*," I explained. "You read it last year when you had Miss Dreyfuss. Remember how Beatrice and Benedick are always mocking each other out, so their friends decide it would be a good trick to turn them into lovers?"

"You'd have more luck with Rory and Lissa if they really were like Beatrice and Benedick," Connor said. He didn't sound bemused any longer. He sounded almost angry. "If they argued with each other, if they appeared to dislike each other, then it would seem that there was some emotion between them. You'd have something to work on, something to turn into love. But what they feel for each other is merely indifference, which is another way of saying nothing at all. Now, how do you make something out of nothing?"

"I refuse to allow you to discourage me," I responded primly. "We'll do just what Beatrice and Benedick's friends did. I'll tell Lissa that Rory likes her, and you'll tell Rory that Lissa likes him."

"And then   ?"

"And then they'll take it from there. You'll see." I spoke with more confidence than I felt. "Let's compose a letter for you to send to Rory."

"I've never written to Rory in my life," Connor protested. "Why would I start now?"

"To tell him the startling news, dummy," I retorted. "To let him know that Lissa is falling for him. The very unexpectedness of your letter will lend weight to what you're saying."

"I won't do it," Connor said. "It's too stupid."

"Connor," I reminded him, "you promised."

He snorted. "We're acting like a pair of twelve year olds. Remember those phone calls, those notes, the whispering during math class? 'Johnny likes you, Susie. Susie likes you, Johnny!' Remember all that stuff?"

"Yeah." I remembered it all right. No one had ever said any of it to me. After all, if I looked twelve now, at twelve I'd looked eight. "We're going to do it anyway. If Hero and Claudio could do it, why can't we? They were a lot older than we are."

"That was four hundred years ago," Connor grumped.

"What does that have to do with it?"

"People stayed kids longer in those days. They were more innocent."

"That's not true," I retorted instantly. "Juliet was thirteen. It says so right in the play."

That shut him up. And then he did have fun writing the letter. We both laughed a lot. By the time we were done, we had composed a fairly decent rough draft. It contained some parts with which I wasn't totally happy, but Connor was remarkably stubborn. The following version is the one for which I was forced to settle:

———————

Dear Rory,

It was great seeing you at the wedding. I was happy for the chance to talk to you about Yale. You got me really interested in the school, and when I come up later this fall to look the place over, I hope I can see you too. (Connor insisted on that part. He said it gave the letter authenticity. I didn't bother to ask him what he meant by that. It didn't do any harm, and if that's what he wanted—well, I de-

———————

cided he ought to have his own way in a few things at least.)

I have to tell you something really funny that happened. I thought it might interest you to hear about it. After your father and Carrie left on their honeymoon, and you left to go back to your own house, most of the guests had drifted away, and I was just sitting around with Mandy and Lissa and my sister, shooting the breeze. And Lissa said, 'I'm beginning to think it's kind of nice that my mother married Peter. Now I'll get to see more of Rory. I think I'd like that.' (I wanted him to say something stronger, but that was as far as he'd go.) *I wouldn't mention that I told you this. Lissa might be mad at me for repeating it. But I thought you might like to hear about it. Knowing might make things better for you when you get together with your father and Carrie and Lissa.*

I'll write to tell you when I'm coming up to Yale. Thanks again for taking all that time to talk to me.

Sincerely,
Connor.

―――――――

"OK," I said when we were done, "now you copy it and send it, and then I'll talk to Lissa."

"Not without me, you don't," Connor in-

―――――――

sisted. "You got to see what I'm writing to Rory. I want to hear what you say to Lissa."

So I told him to come over to have supper with us Friday night. I said I'd bring up the subject then. It would be even better with him there. He could back me up.

Peter and Aunt Carrie were still in Mexico on their honeymoon; my father was off on some tiny island in the Caribbean, which, in addition to the possibility of oil, held nothing but white beaches next to a blue sea and one or two little guest houses. My father's description of it had made it sound like the perfect place to recuperate from the exertions of making a wedding, and my mother planned to stay there with him until he came back. It was the first time Lissa and I had been left alone in the house. We had been, after a lengthy family conference, deemed old enough.

So when Connor came for dinner, it was Lissa and I who prepared the meal. We had tomato soup and a tuna fish casserole and hot buttered garlic toast and a tossed green salad. Connor cleaned his plate three times and praised each item far beyond its worth. It was fun to cook for someone who consumed each morsel with such gusto. "You know, Connor," Lissa said as she served the ice cream and cookies, "you make me feel like Julia Child. It's very flattering."

"You're better than Julia Child," Connor insisted. "Whoever actually tasted anything Julia Child cooked? Maybe all that stuff on TV is made out of plaster of Paris."

Lissa sat down again and began daintily spooning coffee ice cream into her mouth. "You'll have to come more often," she said.

"Yeah, you'll have to come sometimes when your cousin Rory comes," I said. I thought it was time to get down to the business of the evening. "I imagine he'll be eating here a lot after Aunt Carrie and Peter get back."

"Oh, I don't think so," Lissa said lightly. "Why should he? He's away at school for one thing, and for another thing, mostly he's at his mother's house when he's not at school. He and Peter don't really see all that much of each other."

Connor was wolfing down his ice cream, his eyes fixed on the bowl. I kicked him under the table. He looked up at me, startled. "Did you hear that, Connor?" I said sharply. "Did you hear what Lissa said? She doesn't think that Rory will be here too often. I guess she doesn't know."

"Know what?" Lissa sounded worried. "Rory isn't planning to move in here or anything like that is he? I always thought he got along OK with his mother."

Thank heavens Connor was done eating at last. He pushed the bowl away and sighed. "He likes his mother fine," he said. "I'm sure he has no intention of moving in. But don't be surprised if he shows up around here quite a bit. I think he'll be seeing a lot more of his father than he used to."

"Well, why?" Lissa wanted to know. "Just because his father is married? What difference should that make?"

"Oh, it's not really his father he'll be coming to see." Connor was very good at making his voice sound light and casual. "And it certainly won't be your mother." He smiled at her benignly.

"Then who will it be?" Lissa queried. She sounded genuinely confused.

Connor shoved another cookie in his mouth and didn't say a word. He just looked mysterious, or as mysterious as a person can look while chewing chocolate chips.

I stepped into the breach. "Maybe you," I offered.

"Me!" Lissa uttered a short, sharp laugh. "Rory is about as interested in me as I am in him."

"Don't be so sure of that," I said. "I saw his

eyes on you the day of the wedding when you were all on the landing having your picture taken. You didn't notice, because you were looking at the camera the way you were supposed to, but Rory was looking at you."

Connor nodded his agreement. "It's more than just looking, " he said. "Rory told me. . . ." His voice fell off suggestively.

"What did he tell you?" Lissa wanted to know.

The letter had been one thing. It's harder to fib in person. Connor sort of shrugged his shoulders and spread out his hands, vaguely suggesting matters beyond his powers of expression. Once more I was forced to improvise. "He said you were awfully pretty. He said you were just about the best-looking girl he'd ever seen."

"He said that to you?" Lissa sounded utterly unbelieving.

"No, to me," Connor interjected hastily. "I told Mandy about it. I wanted to know if she thought we ought to tell you."

"We kind of debated about it," I said. "We hesitated." If there was a Pulitzer Prize for lying, I would have won it. "We know the situation is kind of awkward. That's why Rory didn't, well, you know, didn't make any moves himself."

"So why are you telling me now?" Lissa's voice was as cool and remote as ever. "I think your first idea, not to tell me, was the best one. The situation *is* awkward. I can't go out with Rory."

"You could if you wanted to," I said.

"But I don't want to." She pulled the ice cream carton toward her. "Do you want some more, Connor?" She was changing the subject.

"Sure," Connor said. He held out his bowl, she took it, filled it with two scoops and passed it back to him.

I was not going to let the subject be changed. "Why don't you want to? He's handsome, and he likes you, and you're not involved with anyone else. I mean, who are you going to go with to the Charity Ball? You better get started on something."

It was a dumb remark, and I knew it. All Lissa had to do was crook her little finger at Stan or Willie or Carl and they'd kill each other for the chance to take her to the ball. Connor shot me a glance that let me know the precise extent of my stupidity. Lissa was kinder. All she said was, "Just because Rory said I'm pretty doesn't mean he wants to go out with me. Someone might say he thinks the Mona Lisa is beautiful. It doesn't mean he wants to go out with her."

"You're not a painting," I retorted.

"Please, Mandy," Lissa said firmly. "Let's not talk about this anymore. I really don't believe Rory is the least bit interested in me, no matter what you claim he said, and I know for sure I'm not the least bit interested in him. More ice cream, Connor?"

"If he eats another drop of ice cream, he'll explode!" I stood up, grabbed the carton and marched into the kitchen to return it to the freezer. A moment later, the swinging door swished back and forth once more, and Connor was in the kitchen with me.

"Hey, what's the big idea?" he complained. "Lissa offered me more ice cream and I want some."

I let the freezer door shut with a bang. "You ought to think about your acne," I said.

"I think about my acne all the time," he shot back. "Why do you think I'm growing the beard? What're you mad at me for anyway? I did my best."

"That was your best? All you could do is agree that Rory thinks Lissa is pretty. Everyone thinks Lissa is pretty. You'd have to be totally blind not to think so."

"Well, what did you want me to say?" He opened the freezer and took out the ice cream.

"That he told you he's nuts about her."

He picked up a spoon from the kitchen table and began eating the ice cream right from the carton. "You wanted me to say something completely unbelievable? Where would that have gotten us? She'd have known it was some kind of trick."

Why did I feel such unreasonable annoyance at Connor's irrefutable reasonableness? I was trying to think of something smart to say next when Lissa called from the dining room, "Hey, you guys, what's the big idea? I don't like drinking my tea all by myself."

Carrying the ice cream carton, Connor returned to the dining room.

I spooned some cat food into a bowl and carried it out to the barn. Retrieving the dish I'd left there the day before, I brought it back into the kitchen and left it in the sink to wash later. Then I pushed open the swinging door between the dining room and the kitchen.

"That's a super idea," I heard Connor say.

"I think it'll make Mandy very happy," Lissa replied in her sweet, clear voice.

"What will make me happy?" I asked as I entered the room. Connor and Lissa were sitting in the same chairs they'd occupied earlier, but

Connor had moved his over so that it practically touched Lissa's. As I spoke, Lissa blushed and Connor looked up, startled. I felt like an intruder.

"Your birthday," Connor said after a brief but noticeable pause. "We were talking about what you'd like for your birthday."

Lissa nodded. "It's going to be a surprise."

"My birthday? My birthday isn't until two days before Christmas."

"This present takes planning," Connor said.

"You've never given me a birthday present in my life, Connor. Except when we were in nursery school together, and you got invited to my parties. And then your mother picked it out— and paid for it too. It was really from her."

"It's *my* present," Lissa explained. "Connor's just helping me."

"You won't even be here for my birthday," I reminded her. "You'll be in Texas with your dad." She always left as soon as school closed for the holidays.

"I'll leave the present behind," she explained. "What's so hard about that?"

"And we're not going to discuss it any further," Connor announced firmly.

"Oh yes, we are," I said. "Come on, you two, tell me what this is really all about."

But for all his apparent amiability, no one could be more stubborn than Connor, as I already knew. He refused to say another word on the subject. Later, I might have pried something more out of Lissa, but after supper Stan Schneiderman and Rob Palowski both showed up, and we spent the rest of the evening listening to them mock each other out. By the time the three guys left, I'd forgotten the whole conversation.

There was nothing to do after that but wait until Connor heard from Rory. I hoped his return letter would give us something more to work with.

It didn't. It was short—pleasant, but short.

———————

Dear Connor,

Thanks for writing to me. I'm glad you're interested in Yale. Why don't you come up and spend a weekend with me and look the place over? Any weekend is OK; just let me know ahead of time which one.

Maybe when I get to know her better, I'll enjoy having Lissa Koerner as a sister. Give my regards to your folks.

Sincerely,
Rory

———————

Connor showed me the letter after school when we were both working in the publications room. We stood talking softly by the window, so no one else could hear us.

"You'll go," I said. "Of course you'll go. And I'll try to get Peter to drive you. I'll tell him it's a good chance for him to visit Rory. And then, somehow, I'll work it so Carrie and Lissa go along too."

"You never give up, do you?" he said. "It sure sounds like a lost cause to me."

I pretended I hadn't heard him. "Maybe I'll go too," I said. "I'd better. It's going to take a lot more effort than I first thought to get these two together."

Connor put his hand on my shoulder. "Mandy, what's this all about?" he asked quietly. "I mean it. This isn't just a game for you. Why are you so set on it?"

"Of course it's just a game," I answered lightly. "I'm making up my own romantic novel, that's all."

"Yeah," Connor replied darkly. "Rory is the hero, but Lissa isn't really the heroine. She's a stand-in for you."

I shivered. Was it possible that he knew me as well as I knew myself—or even better? "Don't be silly," I replied airily. I turned away from him and went back to my desk. He remained at the window for a long time, staring at the band practicing out in the schoolyard. At least, I supposed that's what he was doing. Otherwise, why would he just stand in one spot, his eyes fixed on the distance, when he had so much work to do?

Later that same day, I took supper up to the loft for Trilby and her kittens. They weren't there. I called and called. I looked in every corner, under every tire and rag and dusty piece of abandoned, broken-down furniture. I climbed down and searched under the cars, behind the cars, inside the cars. But I couldn't find them. The next morning, when I inspected the loft before I went to school, I discovered that the bowls of food I'd left there were untouched. The cats were gone.

It was a raw, rainy day, the kind of day for which early November is famous—or infamous, rather—in our part of the country. The fine weather that had held throughout so much of the autumn was gone with one wild blast of the east wind. I walked to school, huddled against the weather in my heavy sweater, raincoat and boots, the wind so strong as to make my umbrella useless. I walked alone. Iggie had driven Lissa in his van. Lissa asked him to take me too, but I didn't want to be the third wheel, not even for five minutes.

If I were late, the cats were my excuse. But I didn't really care if I was late. Now that the cats were gone, I didn't care about anything. I had a superior case of the dismals. The night before, while reading a Georgette Heyer novel in bed, I had actually lifted it up and thrown it against the wall. I was suddenly sick of novels. Nothing suited me. I was all mixed up, like the weather.

That night my parents blew in, and the next day Peter and Carrie came back from their honeymoon, looking just as radiant as they had when they'd left, if a little tired. The storm had delayed their flight home, and they had waited four hours in the Atlanta airport, and it hadn't affected their dispositions at all. Mom and Dad looked great too, tanned and smiling, as if, like Carrie and Peter, they'd just returned from a lovely honeymoon. Well, in a way they had.

I tossed a little guilt in the direction of all four of them, as we sat eating the dinner that Lissa and I had prepared. "We worked hard keeping up with this house while you were away," I said. "And we still had to do all of our schoolwork. Look at us, we're thin and pale as ghosts."

My father's eyes examined my face. "You

look delicious to me, Duchess," he said. "As always."

"We may look pretty good, but if Lissa and I don't get away for a few days, we'll probably come down with mono or something," I informed him briskly.

"You feel all right, Lissa?" Aunt Carrie's glance was full of concern. I think it was the first time she'd looked at Lissa, really looked at her, in six weeks.

Lissa smiled back wanly. "I'm all right," she said in a thin voice. Like me, I guess she was not above turning the screws a notch or two.

"We ought to go somewhere next weekend," I said. "And I know where. Connor is going up to Yale to look over the school. He's staying with Rory. We could drive him up, and then, Peter, you'd have a chance to visit with Rory too."

Lissa looked at me as if I really were sick. "You mean you want all of us to go up to Yale? The whole family? Ugh."

I knew it sounded kind of odd. After all I was almost sixteen and Lissa was almost seventeen. We'd been begging off family weekends for years.

Peter looked doubtful too. "I don't know if

Rory would appreciate all of us descending upon him," he said. "I mean, this whole group could be a little overwhelming. We'd have to take over an entire floor of the Park Sheraton, like an Arab oil sheik and his entourage."

Another flop. Nothing was going right. Between the state of the weather and the state of my mind, that really was no surprise to me.

"Mandy, you go with Connor," Lissa suggested brightly. "Rory will be glad to see you."

"Why don't both of you girls go?" Aunt Carrie chimed in. "I think Rory might enjoy that very much—two lovely ladies to show off to his buddies."

She had forgotten that Yale was full of women now. Lissa would have stood out even in Hollywood, but a girl like me would pass entirely unnoticed. Nevertheless, I grabbed at the straw. "I don't know about Rory, but I'd enjoy it. It's time I started looking at colleges. I could arrange for an interview, like Connor." I turned to Peter. "We wouldn't bother Rory. We'll just have lunch with him one day and give him your regards. Otherwise we'll leave him alone," I lied cheerfully.

"Well, you go ahead with Connor," Lissa insisted. "What do you need me for?"

I was thinking quickly now. "I won't go unless you come too. Connor will be staying with Rory. I don't want to stay in the hotel alone. You come too. We'll go to a football game, and we'll see a show at the Yale Rep. It'll be fun. You need the change too."

"I think it's a wonderful plan, just wonderful," my mother gushed enthusiastically. "If Connor's folks can't spare their car, he can borrow mine."

The white boat. She had it washed twice a week and would sooner lend someone her wedding ring than her Cadillac. But I understood. Even though there were women at Yale, there were still lots of men. She had images of me drawn into a whirl of football games, college parties, smoky evenings in crowded, intimate bars —the kind of social life she thought a daughter of hers ought to have.

"Of course you have nothing to wear," my mother added, "but that's all right. We'll get what you need. We can go shopping tomorrow."

"No, Aunt Mary," Lissa interjected quietly. "I'll go shopping with Mandy. I'll see that she gets the right stuff."

"Oh?" A faint expression of disappointment

could be discerned in my mother's face, but it fled rapidly. "Of course," she agreed. "That would be better."

I shot Lissa a questioning glance, but she just smiled at me blandly. "Then you *are* going," I said to her.

"Yes," she said. "I'm going."

I excused myself from the table early. Mother and Aunt Carrie felt sufficiently guilty at my presentation of Lissa and myself as two over-worked Cinderellas to offer to clean up. I rushed up to the third floor and the hall phone that Lissa and I shared. I had a lot of work to do, fast. I dialed Connor's number as quickly as I could. When I heard his voice on the other end of the wire, I could hardly contain myself. "I fixed it, I fixed it!" I exclaimed excitedly. My gloom had entirely dissipated. It was all going to work out. Deep down in my stomach, where I always received important signals, I could feel it.

"For heaven's sake, Mandy," Connor said, "calm down. What did you fix?"

"Yale. I fixed Yale."

"I didn't know it was broken."

"Connor, I have no time for sophomoric humor," I retorted impatiently. "We're going to Yale. Next weekend. Lissa and me. We're going to go up with you, and my mother said you can take her car."

There was a moment of silence at the other end, and then Connor said slowly, "Next weekend? Next weekend? I guess that will be all right. I guess I can arrange it. The only thing is, I have to check with Rory. I have to make sure it's all right with him."

"It better be," I said. "I've got everyone all hyped up. I don't know if I can do that again. I told them you were already planning to go up next weekend. It sounded more realistic that way."

"Well, now what'll we do?" Connor said, his voice more than a little cross. "What'll we do if it's not all right with Rory? What'll we do then?"

"Oh, Connor," I protested, "you have no imagination." My new-found joy was not to be dimmed. "I'll think of something. I'll say you came down with a cold and had to change your plans. It won't be a problem."

"I'll have to arrange for an interview," he said thoughtfully. "I can do that tomorrow."

"Me too," I said. "Do you think they'll interview juniors?"

"I don't see why not," Connor said. "But if you can't get one, and you like the looks of the place, and you're really serious about applying, you can always go back for an interview next year."

"Yeah," I agreed. "Anyway, it's not important. What's important is that I hang up so you can call Rory and straighten all this out with him."

"Right, boss," Connor replied smartly. "I'll call you back."

He did, fifteen minutes later, to say that it was fine with Rory. He said whatever he was doing the following weekend, Connor could just do it along with him.

"What about us?" I said. "Did you tell him Lissa and I were coming too?"

"Yes. I told him you and Lissa were staying at the hotel. I said you two wouldn't get in our way, you intended to go about your own business, but were taking this opportunity to drive up with me."

"Why did you say a thing like that?" I protested. "I intend for us to spend every minute we can with him."

"Well, kiddo," Connor explained, "when I told him you guys were coming up too, he didn't exactly sound overcome by joy. I had to kind of reassure him that it would be all right."

"Geez," I murmured. "Do you suppose

since the wedding he's gotten himself a girl friend?" Suddenly things didn't feel so right in my stomach anymore. And why hadn't I considered that possibility before? After all, I knew as well, if not better, than anyone else that a guy who looked like Rory was not likely to remain unattached long. "Trilby and her kittens have disappeared," I grumbled. "I should have known that was a sign."

"When did you turn superstitious?" Connor queried sharply.

"I'm only superstitious when it comes to cats," I assured him.

"Well, I'm sorry about Trilby and the kittens, but you know perfectly well they have nothing to do with Rory and his girl friends, or his non-girl friends," Connor lectured. "We'll know what's what when we get up there. We'll just have to play it by ear."

I knew that what he said was true. The whole thing was turning out to be much more complicated than I'd ever dreamed. Claudio and Hero didn't have anything like so much trouble with Beatrice and Benedick. But I wasn't ready to give up. I wasn't ready to suggest to Connor that he'd won the bet. Besides, no matter what happened, a weekend at Yale was bound to be interesting.

Even if Lissa and I went to a football game and out to dinner and to the theater just with each other, we'd have fun. I wasn't going to be gloomy any more. It didn't pay.

Chapter Five

AFTER SCHOOL the next day Lissa took me shopping. She wouldn't even let my mother drive us to town. She said we'd take the bus. "Why?" I asked her as we stood on the corner shivering while we waited for one of the creaking vehicles left over from the Spanish-American War, which in Winter Hill came along no more than once in an hour. The sun was shining, and the east wind had shifted to the north, clearing the air but doing nothing to improve the temperature. "Why wouldn't you let my mother drive us to town? Why do we have to stand here and freeze?"

"You know if she'd driven us, she couldn't have resisted coming into the stores," Lissa said, shoving mittened hands deep into her jacket pockets. "When you shop with your mother, it turns out all wrong."

"When I shop with anyone, it turns out all wrong," I retorted. I had tried very hard to convince Lissa that my usual jeans and T-shirts would do perfectly well at Yale, but she had said that if I wouldn't come shopping with her, she wouldn't go to Yale with me.

"How do you know?" Lissa asked. "You've never shopped with anyone but your mother. She has this idea of what she thinks you ought to look like. I guess it's more or less what she and my mother looked like when they were girls. Well, it doesn't suit you. We have to remember that your father calls you 'Duchess.'"

"He doesn't mean anything. It's just a joke."

Lissa shook her head. "No, it's not a joke. There is something aristocratic about your looks. Something classical."

I was too startled to come up with a sensible retort. Blessedly, the bus came along at just that moment, and I climbed in silently, turning over in my mind what Lissa had just said. When we were seated, our mufflers unwound, and our hats removed, I threw another question at her. "Listen," I said, "why are you taking me shopping? Why are you doing me this big favor? I mean, last time my mother made you come. This time you volunteered."

Lissa patted my arm. "Oh, I have my reasons," she said with a little smile. "Besides, I like to shop. I like to shop for me, and it's fun to shop for someone else too. But the time we went for that chiffon dress, my mind was a million miles away. You remember how I was right before the wedding."

"Yes," I said. "I'm glad you're feeling better."

"What's done is done," Lissa replied calmly. "It's like the divorce itself. You get used to it after a while. You'd better."

"Yeah, I guess so," I agreed.

"But anyway, I was so out of it, I let your mother buy you that blue tutu. You looked like an overgrown elf."

I grinned. "That's putting it in the kindest way possible. I thought I looked like one of those circus monkeys they dress up as ballet dancers."

Lissa nodded. "When I was able to think about someone else besides myself again, I felt guilty about that. I should never have let Aunt Mary buy that dress for you. I could have stopped her."

"It doesn't matter," I reassured her. "No dress would have been the right dress."

Lissa shook her head firmly. "That's just not true," she said. "You'll see."

We didn't go into Grace Crawford's. We didn't go into Kids 'N' Things either. We went into a shop called Village Green. Lissa had to literally drag me through the door. "This is a preppy place," I protested. "I'm not a preppy. I think I'm more of an alligator."

"When you shop for yourself you can buy for yourself an entire outfit made out of slimy green scales," Lissa said. "When you shop with me, you'll do what I tell you."

I was surprised to hear Lissa attempt a wise-crack. I had to laugh, and by the time I was done I found myself inside a dressing room, the door shut, and my pants and my shirt removed and carried off by Lissa to the front of the store so that I couldn't escape if I wanted to. "I'll pick out the stuff," were her parting words. "You just wait here."

I wrapped myself in my parka, which Lissa had graciously left behind, and jumped around on the dressing room carpet for what must have been half an hour in a futile attempt to keep my legs and my butt warm. I almost began to believe that Lissa, overcome by a secret yen to be me, had absconded with my overalls and my flannel shirt.

But she returned to the dressing room at last, followed by a saleswoman. Both were burdened down with skirts, shirts, wool dresses, even socks and scarfs. Lissa left nothing to chance.

Every time I opened my mouth, she told me to shut up. She said she had no time for conversation, she had to concentrate. She concentrated, like Edison inventing the electric light. She put more sheer energy into outfitting me than she had into anything else I'd ever seen her do. In less than an hour she'd fitted me out with two pleated skirts, three sweaters, three shirts, three pairs of knee socks to match the sweaters, a pocketbook, a clingy pale green wool dress with a turtle neck, and a blazer. She spent six hundred dollars. The only thing that saved me from a heart attack when I saw the bill was the fact that I'd already seen the price tags on each of the garments. Lissa didn't even bat an eye. She just handed over one of my mother's charge cards and watched silently while the ecstatic saleswoman rang up the sale.

"This is terrible," I said. "Tomorrow I'm bringing half these things back."

"Your mother said I could spend a thousand dollars if I had to," Lissa replied calmly.

The saleswoman's head jerked up like a puppet's. "Can I show you something else?" she asked. "Lingerie? Some belts? We're having a sale on outerwear."

"This is fine," I said hastily. "Just fine."

"Jewelry?" the woman suggested. "You'll need a stick pin for the blazer."

"She has plenty of jewelry," Lissa said.

It was true. I'd been receiving really good things on my birthday and Christmas for several years. I just never wore them.

Outside the store, I was able to breathe again. I felt I had just escaped from the center of a whirlwind. But Lissa wasn't done with me, not by a long shot. She was so elated she seemed to be floating. "I knew it," she crowed. "I knew it. We got you just your kind of thing. Neat, smart, put together, but not too much. This style suits your looks and it suits your personality. Once I knew what to do, it didn't take any time at all. It's just a matter of knowing who a person really is." She smiled a smile of smug self-congratulation. "I am a genius. I should go into the business. Maybe I will," she added thoughtfully. "When you're a famous journalist or editor, you can send all your friends who're too busy to shop for themselves to me. I'll take care of them."

"I bet you will," I murmured under my breath.

If she heard me, she ignored the remark. "We're going in here now," she said, turning sharply toward a shop door.

I stopped and looked up at the sign. Were we where I thought we were? Indeed we were. The sign read: "Hairafter: Unisex Salon." "Hey, wait a minute!" I balked at last. "I don't need to spend good money on a haircut. When I need one, my mother just takes off an inch or two around the edges."

Lissa let go of the door, which she'd already pushed open, and turned toward me. "Mandy," she said firmly, "listen to me."

"Yes, boss," I replied, enacting meekness.

"I'm serious, Mandy. You complain that everyone takes you for about twelve. I think that's the way you really want it."

"I can't help being short," I replied, stung. "I don't like it."

"Mandy, it has nothing to do with being short," Lissa shot back. "You want to look sixteen, come in here and have a haircut. You want to look twelve, go home, leave your hair in pigtails and never as long as you live utter one more word of complaint about being handed a pencil box when you buy a pair of shoes. It's up to you. It's your choice. You have to decide how long you're going to go on hiding."

When she put it like that, what could I do? I pushed in front of her, opened the door, and entered the shop. The decor was all mirrors and disco lights. The receptionist, a dead ringer for Farrah Fawcett, stared at me as if I were something her cat had dug out of the garbage, if she had a cat, which I doubt. "Can I help you?" she asked, implying by her tone of voice that I was beyond anyone's assistance. I have to admit that places like Hairafter made me faintly paranoid. That's an understatement. They scared the hell out of me.

I turned back toward the door. Lissa was blocking the way. "She wants a haircut," Lissa said. "If Timothy is here, we'll take him."

"Timothy is busy," Farrah said coldly.

"We'll wait," Lissa said, equally coldly.

"Is that you, Lissa darling?" a voice called from the back of the shop. A thin, blond man in a bright red jumpsuit hurried toward us out of the gloom.

"Hi, Timothy," Lissa said. "I brought you my cousin. You know, the one I told you about, with the gorgeous hair."

I looked around. "Which cousin is that?"

"You're a card too," Timothy said, rubbing the end of my braid through expert fingers.

"Timothy, you have an appointment with Mrs. Gleason in five minutes," Farrah complained.

"Mrs. Gleason can wait," Timothy returned. "You come with me, honey." His eyes gleamed.

"You must be new here," Lissa said to Farrah. "Otherwise you'd know by now that Timothy can't resist a challenge."

Timothy escorted me to a little booth where the light was as bright and revealing as it was dim and sexy in the reception area. He sat me in a barber's chair, wrapped me up like a mummy in a smock and a rubber cape, and stared silently at my reflection in the mirror for what seemed like an hour, but was, I suppose, no more than five minutes. Then he nodded, and left. A moment later a young woman came in and washed my hair, gossiping pleasantly while she rubbed and scrubbed. I didn't answer her because my teeth were chattering. I didn't know where Lissa had gone. Apparently, she had deserted me. Heaven alone knew what was going to happen to me now. I suspected medieval torture.

When my hair had been thoroughly soaped, rinsed, resoaped and creamed and rinsed again, Timothy returned. "Ready?" he asked. He sounded like a surgeon. It was with difficulty that I resisted requesting an anesthetic.

Unlike the young woman, Timothy didn't say a word while he worked. He really was like a surgeon, or at least like surgeons are on TV soap operas. He was fast too. In twenty minutes it was all done, not just the cutting, but also the blow-drying. Not until the job was complete did I notice a flicker of expression on Timothy's face. But when he held a mirror up behind me, I could see his lips break into a smile. "Well," he said, "how do you like it?"

I stared at the face reflected in the mirror. It was small, with a pointed chin and large blue eyes. An aureole of short-cropped black curls framed it delicately. I knew the face was mine. And yet it was not a face that I'd ever seen before.

"I don't know," I squeaked. "I don't know what I think."

"You'll get used to it," he said. He didn't sound a bit insulted. In fact, he sounded supremely satisfied, like Lissa when we'd come out of the Village Green. "It's always a shock the first time you realize that you're good-looking. But you must have suspected."

Had I? Had I been hiding, as Lissa had claimed? I murmured, "Thank you, Timothy." In a daze, I left the little booth and made my way to the front of the shop.

Lissa was still there. She hadn't deserted me. They had made her sit in the waiting room. They never let loved ones watch the actual operation.

She stood up as I walked toward her. "Oh, Mandy," she exclaimed softly, "it's perfect. It's better than I dreamed it would be. Mandy, you're beautiful."

"You're prejudiced," I said, with an attempt at levity.

"I agree with Lissa," Timothy said. I hadn't realized he was behind me.

"And you have a vested interest in me now too," I retorted, turning toward him. "You certainly can't be classed as an objective observer."

He smiled. "That'll be twenty dollars."

Lissa opened her purse and pulled out the money. She'd come prepared for this too. "Timothy, you're a genius," she said.

"I know," he responded.

"You're using that word very freely today," I commented.

"Once you're used to yourself, you'll agree with us," Lissa said. "Come on, let's go home. I can't wait to show you off to my mother and yours. I'll sneak you up the back steps, and when you come down for supper, wear one of your new outfits—the pink and green tweed skirt with the green sweater and the pink blouse, I think," she said. "Unless you prefer that Stuart plaid."

"I don't prefer anything." My head felt strangely light, as if I'd been walking around for years like the Man in the Iron Mask, and suddenly the helmet had been removed.

My mother and Aunt Carrie were just as excited as Lissa had anticipated. They crowed over me as if I were a newborn baby.

I told myself not to believe them either. After all, they were prejudiced too. They were my mother and my aunt. But I smiled at their compliments and said, "Thank you." I couldn't help it.

I refused to wear any of my new clothes to school. But I had to wear my new hairdo. About seven different girls told me they liked it. And in English class I had to walk right by Claudio and Benedick, otherwise known as Steve Ellery and Bruno Kruczek, to get to my seat.

They watched me come down the aisle. Bruno held up his hand like a traffic cop. I stopped. "Hi, Bruno," I said.

"Hi, Mandy," he responded.

"Hi, Mandy," Steve echoed.

They had never stopped me before. I don't think they'd ever even said hello to me before, though of course I'd always known them. I glanced from Bruno's face to Steve's and then back to Bruno's again.

"Today I'm going to tell Miss Dreyfuss that

you should read Beatrice," Bruno said. "You'll be able to do it better than Gillie Stedman. She sounds like a telephone operator."

"Yeah," Steve agreed. "You're more the Beatrice type."

"I am?" I laughed. "It's OK with me. I don't mind."

Then, after school, in the publication room, Connor came up to me. "Cripes, kiddo, what did you do with yourself?" he asked. "I mean, you've always been pretty, but today you look fantastic."

I had always been pretty. An interesting remark. But it was only Connor talking. "Thanks, chum," I said. "I had my hair cut for Yale. You know, I did arrange an interview. I couldn't look twelve any more."

"I never thought you were twelve," he said softly.

"No, of course not," I replied. "You've known me since nursery school. You know how old I am."

"Connor!" It was Miss Dreyfuss calling. "We need you on this, Connor."

"I'll see you," Connor said.

Of course he'd see me. He saw me nearly every day. Maybe he meant the trip. "Yes," I said. "Lissa will drive the car over to your house Friday afternoon. Ask for an early dismissal so you can go home at one and get your stuff. We'll pick you up about two."

"Yeah," Connor said. Still he stood there, staring at me, as if there were something more he wanted to say, something that for the moment he couldn't remember.

"Connor!" the peremptory voice ordered again. Without another word, he turned and walked toward Miss Dreyfuss's desk on the other side of the room.

Chapter Six

 TRAFFIC was heavy driving up to New Haven. What was normally a two and a half hour trip required more than three on a Friday afternoon. Lissa and Connor sat in front taking turns driving. I sat in back, reading.

Henrietta's reflection led her to the mirror and caused her to stare long at her own image.

It should have comforted her. Dark ringlets framed a charming countenance in which two speaking eyes of blue became gradually filled with tears that obscured her vision of a short, straight nose, a provocative upper lip, and an elusive dimple. These attributes had apparently failed to captivate the Viscount.

Soon, however, I had to put the book away. Reading in a moving car tends to make me sick to my stomach.

I leaned forward to catch the animated conversation going on between Lissa and Connor. They were talking about, of all things, cars. Since I didn't know anything about cars, I had to keep quiet. Lissa told Connor that she was working on Aunt Carrie. She was hoping for a car for a high school graduation present. Connor said the only way he'd ever have a car was to earn the money with which to buy one. He had a part-time job at McDonalds, but he was afraid to spend the money he made on a second-hand car because he might need it for college. He would wait to see what kind of scholarships he won. But if he had his choice, if he could buy any kind of car in the whole world, he'd own a Maserati. Lissa, on the other hand, preferred a Mercedes, but admitted that she'd contentedly settle for a Honda.

They chattered on in much this vein all the rest of the way to New Haven. I thought the conversation exquisitely boring, but Lissa, when we finally exited from the Connecticut Turnpike, commented that the time had passed amazingly quickly.

"We'll go to the hotel," Connor said. "I'll drop you and the car, and I'll walk or hop a bus over to Rory's college."

This was not the first time it seemed to me that Connor was forgetting the point of this entire expedition. "That's silly," I commented. "We'll drop you at Rory's college and then we'll drive to the hotel. That'll save you a lot of trouble."

"Yes, that makes much more sense," Lissa said. For once, she was playing into my hands.

We stopped the car and asked a couple of kids on the street how to get to Rory's building. It was my idea that once there, I'd suggest we all run up and say hello to Rory. But I was foiled again. There was no place to park the car anywhere near his college. We'd have had to walk at least a dozen blocks from a garage back to Rory's rooms.

"I'll go with Connor to park the car," I suggested. "You run up to Rory's room, and we'll meet you there."

Lissa balked. "That's dumb. Connor will drive me to the hotel, while you run up to Rory's to tell him we're here. He'd die of embarrassment if we all traipsed through his door anyhow. I'll meet you back at the hotel. I'll register, and you can come back to the hotel whenever you feel like it."

"Oh, that's a good idea," I enthused. "Except for one thing. *You* go up to tell Rory we're here, and *I'll* drive to the hotel with Connor to register." I tapped Connor on the shoulder. "Right, Connor?"

"Not right, Connor," Lissa insisted.

Connor didn't say anything. He was turning out to be impossible. He wasn't helping at all. It certainly had been stupid of me to imagine that someone who'd bet against you would assist you in winning, even if that someone went around assuring you how good he was at keeping promises. "Don't you hear me, Connor?" I urged.

"I'll drop both of you, and the car, at the hotel," Connor said. "Then I'll go back to Rory's college. I'm the one who's sleeping there."

I was going to have to do this alone. "All right," I agreed reluctantly. "But when you find Rory, ask him to have dinner with us. Tell him it's my treat. He's probably tired of cafeteria food anyway. Phone us at the hotel and tell us what he says. We'll wait to hear from you.

Connor guided the car into the driveway of the Park Sheraton. "I'll call you within the hour," he said. "I don't much feature cafeteria food myself."

"Well, all right," Lissa said. "We'll all have dinner together." I sighed with relief. "For your sake, Connor," Lissa added. "I wouldn't want you to collapse from food poisoning." She grinned, pleased with her own unaccustomed wit. And then he grinned, his white teeth gleaming through his red beard. It was full and curly now, the beard of his dreams. You couldn't even notice any longer that he had acne, or that his cheeks were really as hollow as a mummy's.

An attendant took the car. With his knapsack strapped to his shoulders, Connor hurried off to find Rory. Lissa and I registered and followed a porter to our room. As soon as he'd pocketed his tip and disappeared, we kicked off our shoes and lay down on our beds. We were tired. We'd been moving steadily since six-thirty that morning without stopping.

Of the two of us, Lissa should have been the wearier. She'd done a lot of the driving. But she didn't shut her eyes. She wanted to talk. "Mandy . . ." Her voice was soft, hesitant. "Do you mind if I tell you something? Give you a little advice?"

"So far your advice has been all right," I admitted. In a week, I'd gotten used to my new haircut. So had everyone at home and at school. No one said anything about it anymore. I looked sixteen, that's all—but that alone was worth a good deal.

"I don't want you to be insulted. I speak as your friend," Lissa continued.

"I have bad breath."

She giggled. "I wouldn't know. I've never kissed you." Another joke from Lissa. What was going on here? Were we trading places? If she was turning into the witty one, did that mean I was turning into the beautiful one?

But immediately she was serious again. "Mandy, if you want to get Rory interested in you, you can't be too obvious. When we go out tonight, don't insist on buying his dinner, or anything like that. You have to be more subtle, or you'll scare him off."

At first I was too startled to reply. "You see?" she said sadly. "I've hurt your feelings. I was afraid of that. I didn't mean to."

"No, no," I hurried to assure her. "You didn't hurt my feelings at all. I appreciate your advice. I really do. You know so much more about these things than I do. Only . . ." Now what was I to say?

"Only what?"

"I'm not interested in Rory one bit," I improvised. "Not the way you mean. I just want to be, well, cousinly to him, that's all. I just want to act like he's part of our family, so he won't be sorry any more that his father married your mother. You have to admit we have a pretty terrific family. I mean, we're something good to be a part of."

"It's a pretty overwhelming family, too," Lissa said. "The Cobbs of Winter Hill. That takes some getting used to."

"The Cobbs of Winter Hill," I echoed, but my tone was ironic. "Winter Hill is not New York City. The Cobbs are not the Rockefellers."

"How did we get on this subject?" Lissa asked. "It's not what we were talking about."

"We were talking about how I'm not one bit interested in Rory Ramussen, not in that way, not, you know, as a man." What a lie. But it was in a good cause. The Lord would forgive me. "It's you who should be interested in him. He likes you."

"What a bunch of garbage," Lissa scoffed.

"He told Connor he thinks you're pretty."

"When we're together, he doesn't even glance at me!" Lissa exclaimed. "He doesn't know what I look like."

"But Connor said . . ."

"Connor didn't say it," Lissa reminded me. "You said it. I don't know what that was all about. I think you have a bad case of Rory on the brain."

"I AM NOT interested in Rory Ramussen," I shouted.

She looked at me, her eyebrows raised in a question. "No? OK. If that's the way you want to play it, I'll go along." She lay her head down in the middle of two plump pillows, one piled on top of the other. A sly little smile played about her lips as she shut her eyes. I knew she didn't believe me. I knew she was convinced that I was in love with Rory myself. I could deny it until I was blue in the face, and she still wouldn't believe me.

She wouldn't believe me at least in part because none of my denials would quite ring true. And maybe that wasn't entirely a bad thing. If she thought she was helping me to sink my own hooks into Rory, she wouldn't object so much to our spending time with him. And I didn't doubt for one second that once she and Rory had spent a few hours together in a relaxed, unpressured atmosphere, they would recognize in each other their destined mate, or at least their destined date for the Charity Ball. And once that had happened, I didn't think I'd have much difficulty convincing Lissa of the sincerity of my claim to utter disinterest in Rory Ramussen.

I too shut my eyes. I guess we both drifted

off. My sleep was light, restless, full of dreams. I dreamed I was at the Charity Ball myself. I knew it was the Charity Ball, but the women were all wearing the high-waisted Empire dresses of the Regency, and the men were in scarlet-coated uniforms. My partner's name was Fitzwilliam Darcy. He had a red beard, like Connor's. I told him no, I couldn't dance with him because I was supposed to be dancing with Rory Ramussen. He was terribly polite and said of course he would help me find my proper partner. A whole row of gentlemen were lined up along the wall, and we went from one to the other, but none of them was Rory. We couldn't find Rory anywhere, but we found Trilby. She and her kittens were sleeping underneath a thin-legged gilt chair. Lissa wasn't in the dream at all.

A bell rang, and Mr. Darcy told me it was time to go in for supper. The insistent clangor of the bell continued, and I awoke. It was no early nineteenth century dinner bell I was hearing, but a thoroughly modern telephone bell. Lissa had awakened before me, and picked up the receiver. "OK," I heard her say as I swam up out of sleep, "eight o'clock at the Dandelion. See you there. So long." Then, as she placed the receiver back on the hook, she directed her attention to me.

"We fell asleep," she said. "Both of us. What time is it?"

I glanced at my watch. "Seven-thirty. Yeah, I guess we really were beat."

"We're supposed to meet Connor and Rory at a restaurant around the corner in half an hour. We'd better get a move on." She leaped out of bed as she spoke. Even though she had fallen asleep in her clothes, she looked entirely unwrinkled. She ran her fingers through her hair, and it too fell immediately into place. It was like magic.

"You don't have to do a thing." I said. "You look fine just the way you are."

"Don't be ridiculous. I'll get in the shower first, and then while you're in the shower I can make up, and then I can help you." In two seconds she had us organized like an army. "But don't rush," she admonished. "If they have to wait five minutes for us, it won't kill them."

But of course we did rush, and by five after eight she had us both fully dressed, coiffed, made-up and out on the street. She wouldn't let me wear the turtle-necked wool dress. She said that had to be saved for Saturday night. "It really shows off your figure," she said. "Tonight we'll come on easy." She sounded like a general planning a campaign.

"You got it all wrong, Lissa," I remonstrated, but weakly. "You don't understand."

"What don't I understand? Wear the blue cord pants and that white silk blouse and some gold chains." The pants were about the only thing from my old wardrobe that had passed her muster. She made up my eyes, put rouge on my sallow cheeks and gloss on my lips. She worked quickly, with deft hands, and it was all done in about five minutes. I was amazed. I had always thought all that stuff took half your life. Sometimes it did, for her, when she had the time. But she could hurry if she needed to. Looking at the finished product, you'd have never guessed it.

The Dandelion was one of those glassy places hung with plants whose menus seem to consist chiefly of things made out of tofu, mushrooms, bean sprouts and zucchini. It struck me as an odd place for Connor, but when the hostess escorted us to a booth, we found him happily ensconced opposite Rory, drinking beer. Rory was sipping one of those clear bubbly liquids with twists of lemon or lime that he appeared to favor.

As soon as Rory caught sight of us, he stood up. "Hi, girls," he said, smiling. "Good to see you." He sounded as if he meant it, though with

Rory it could be hard to tell, because he was so unfailingly polite. "Lissa, you look terrific."

"Thanks, Rory," she replied coolly.

"Please, Lissa, sit down." He had stepped out of the booth and gestured to the seat next to the window. She glanced briefly at Connor and then slid into the place Rory had indicated. Rory sat down next to her. I sat down next to Connor.

"Hey, Mandy," Rory said, "you look terrific too. You did something," he added with a faintly puzzled expression. "I'm not sure what."

"It's my hair," I summarized. "I'm glad you like it."

A waitress asked us what we'd like to drink. Lissa and I both ordered Cokes.

"You shouldn't drink Coke," Rory remonstrated. "It'll ruin your teeth and your stomach. There's also some experimental evidence that caffeine is damaging to the reproductive system. Coke is loaded with caffeine."

"Really, Rory," Lissa commented acidly, "I don't think one Coke will do either Mandy or me any harm."

"It isn't one Coke that I'm concerned about," Rory said in a low, serious voice, turning toward her and holding her eyes with his. "It's all the ones that come after the first one. I'd hate to see you hurt yourself, Lissa." His face was close to hers, their shoulders touching. She shrank back into the corner of her seat and turned her head toward Connor.

"Hey, Connor, how come he let you have a beer?" she asked, with a high, nervous giggle.

"A beer or two may be less harmful than Coke," Rory said. "I have a beer now and then myself. Of course, a beer guzzler is in for trouble. Moderation is the key." The expression in his large brown eyes managed somehow to be sweet and dazzling at the same time.

The waitress set the Cokes down in front of Lissa and me. Lissa reached for hers. Rory's hand stretched in the same direction at the very same moment. I don't know what he was after—the Coke, Lissa's arm, or simply an effective gesture. But the result was that their hands collided, the full glass was knocked over, and the black fizzing liquid spilled in all directions on the table top.

"Oh, cripes, Rory!" Lissa exclaimed, pulling back against the booth as far as she could. "Now look what you've done."

"I'm sorry. I'm terribly sorry." Rory was on his feet, grabbing for napkins with which to sop up the mess before it dripped into our laps.

I stood up, too. There were only four napkins on our table. I walked over to the next one to get some more. Connor also rose, a moment too late. Dark blotches of Coke had already stained his jeans.

"I'm sorry. I'm so sorry," Rory repeated, desperately reaching across the table with the by now useless mush the paper napkins scrunched in his hand had become. At that moment the waitress rescued him with a terry cloth dish towel. Briskly, she successfully completed the mopping up.

Though Rory directed his apologies to Lissa, she said nothing. I really couldn't stand the way she was behaving. After all, however much he might object to Coca-Cola, he hadn't knocked the glass over on purpose. At least not consciously. I touched his sleeve. "It's all right, Rory, really it is," I said. "No harm done. The only person who got wet was Connor, and when the stains dry, you won't even notice them."

"That's right," Connor agreed. "Come on, let's forget about it. Let's have dinner. I'm hungry."

"Sit down, Connor," Lissa said, patting the seat beside her. "I'm going to order another Coke, and I don't want to upset Rory again. It's too dangerous."

I slid into the seat opposite Lissa. "Actually, Lissa, the spill was as much your fault as his."

Rory sat down next to me. "It's nice of you to say that, Mandy, but really it isn't true. It was entirely my fault."

I patted his hand. "Rory, you're making a mountain out of a molehill. Let's just forget the whole business." His face still wore such a stricken expression that I felt the need to divert him. "Really I didn't know that Coke was so dangerous. Where did you hear about that?"

"I keep up with that kind of thing," Rory returned. "I read magazines like *Nutrition* and *Today's Health*."

Connor turned to Lissa. "You know what we saw on our way over here? A Packard from the early twenties. Gorgeous. In perfect shape."

"Wow!" Lissa responded.

"Just out there driving on the street," Connor added.

"I love classic cars," Lissa said. "Of course, you have to have a regular car to drive around in. If I owned a twenties Packard, I would never take it on the road just like that—"

"No, no," Connor interrupted. "That's what I admired. If you have classic cars, you should use them. The whole point of them is that they be in good running condition—"

"Naturally." Now Lissa interrupted Connor. "But that doesn't mean you drive them to the supermarket. Can you imagine what would happen to that Packard in the Foodtown parking lot?"

I had never known that Lissa cared about old cars. I had known she wanted a car of her own, but I had thought that was just the normal human desire for the freedom that's provided by a set of wheels. When I got my license, I'd want a car too, I was sure. But that's all a car was to me—a mode of transportation. It wasn't a topic of dinner table conversation.

I turned toward Rory. "I think cars are boring," I said in a loud whisper.

If either Connor or Lissa heard that remark, they chose to ignore it. Rory smiled at me, a smile as rare and dazzling as sunlight on the snow. "I left my car home," he said. "It's too hard and too expensive to park it around here. I brought my bike. Bicycling is excellent exercise, you know. It's really been keeping me in shape. I don't get as much exercise up here as I should. I should be running. When the weather turns nice again, I will. What's your exercise?"

"Exercise?"

"Yes. What do you do to keep in shape? To stay healthy?"

I grimaced. "Well, I walk to school every morning. That's half a mile."

Rory's smile had disappeared. "Mandy, Mandy, walking half a mile is nothing. That doesn't count. You want to turn flabby? You want to have a heart attack? Or a stroke?"

"I'm only sixteen," I murmured. "Can't I start worrying about all that when I'm seventeen?"

He ignored my attempt at levity. "What do you eat?" he queried sharply.

"What do I eat?"

"Yes, yes," Rory insisted. "What do you eat? Let's start with breakfast. What's your usual breakfast?"

"A cup of coffee and a doughnut," I whispered. I could have lied, but although I knew coffee and doughnuts were wrong, I wasn't sure what was right. I didn't know if he was one of your fiber freaks, your cholesterol counters or your plain old garden variety carbohydrate calculators. If I'd said "bran flakes," I'd have won if he were the first, but lost if he were the last. The simplest thing to do was tell the truth and let him take it from there.

Which he did, right through the dinner he insisted on ordering for me. While Lissa and Connor guzzled beer and Coke, and chomped on the closest thing to human food on the menu, some kind of vegetarian pizza, I dined on bean sprouts, a frozen yogurt shake and tofu. If there hadn't been a large pile of whole wheat pita bread in the middle of the table, I'd have gotten up as hungry as I'd sat down.

Rory explained how in his youth he had suffered from colds, strep throats, and every other kind of childhood ailment with depressing regularity. He had been skinny and frail, out of school half the time and miserable the other half because he was such a failure at sports and the butt of endless teasing. Sick of life as a ninety-seven pound weakling, and under the influence of a concerned gym teacher, he took up body building, good nutrition and healthful living with a vengeance when he was a sophomore in high school. By the time he was a senior, he won the county cross-country championship. He described his exercise regimen, his diet, his course of vitamins, his limited choice among restaurants, and his extensive research into human physiology. I learned about his pulse, his blood pressure, his muscle tone and his basal metabolism. I thought it my great good luck that he resisted the temptation to expound upon his bowel movements.

Out of the corner of my eye, and the corner

of my ear, I realized that Connor and Lissa were as engrossed as Rory and I, or to be more accurate, as Rory and himself. I caught phrases now and then that revealed they had left cars and moved on to more interesting subjects, like movies, the weaknesses and stupidities of various mutual acquaintances, and the intolerable interference in their lives of their respective parents. Lissa laughed a lot, while Connor's eyes shone, and his white teeth gleamed through his beard.

After supper, we meandered around the campus. Rory pointed out the important sights. Somehow I once more ended up next to him, while Connor and Lissa strolled side by side behind us. No one else was interested in switching. Connor and Lissa appeared satisfied with each other's company, and Rory obviously preferred to walk with me. When he was not acting as tour guide, he wanted to continue his lecture on how to live to be a hundred and ten, running all the way. Connor wasn't helping. He wasn't helping one bit. He seemed to have totally forgotten the entire purpose of our trip and stuck to Lissa like a Siamese twin. It was three against one, so naturally I lost. Since I certainly wasn't listening to Rory, only murmuring at appropriate moments little syllables like "Yes," and "Really?" and "Imagine that," I was perfectly able to work out in my head all the terrible accusations I was going to hurl at Connor concerning his feckless faithlessness.

When I heard a clock in a tower strike eleven, I decided I'd had enough. With a huge yawn I succeeded in interrupting Rory's detailed description of a whooping cough attack he'd suffered through at the age of seven.

"You're tired," he noticed. "That's because you don't exercise enough. It's a mistake to think that exercise wears you out. In the long run, it has precisely the opposite effect."

"I'm tired because I got up at six-thirty this morning," I retorted sharply. "It's a good enough reason."

Rory put his arm around my shoulder. "Gee, Mandy, I'm sorry," he said. "Of course it's been a long day for you and Lissa. I apologize for being so thoughtless. It's just that I've been enjoying myself so much, I'd kind of lost track of the time."

"Well, I'm glad you didn't let the spilled Coke ruin it for you," I returned. "It really was sweet of you to spend so much time with three little kids from home."

"Oh, I don't think of you as a little kid, Mandy."

He didn't? That was a change from the day of the wedding.

His hand squeezed my shoulder. "You're great company," he said. "You're lots of fun."

"I am?" How could he possibly know? I hadn't gotten two sentences in edgewise all evening.

"And you aren't so tough on the eyes either," he added.

"Neither are you." That at least was the truth.

"We'll go to the game together tomorrow," he said. "The four of us. Afterwards there's a party at my college."

It was turning into just the kind of weekend my mother had dreamed about for me. So why didn't I feel delighted? Maybe because it wasn't precisely the weekend *I* had dreamed about. "Lissa and I thought maybe we'd go over to the Yale Rep or the Long Wharf tomorrow night," I said.

He shook his head firmly. "You'll never get tickets to either of them on a Saturday night. We'll go out to dinner and then to the party, and if that's no good we'll go someplace else. The four of us. We'll have a chance to talk. You can't talk at the theater."

He'd have a chance to talk. But all right. At least that was what I'd planned—the four of us spending the whole of Saturday together. I didn't even have to bring it up myself. I didn't even have to force the issue. But the infallible signals issuing from my stomach let me know that the four of us spending the day together was not going to turn out as I had imagined.

Chapter Seven

LISSA unlocked the door of our hotel room, grinning like a Cheshire cat. Without saying a word, I entered and began undressing. She followed, not even noticing my silence. "You see?" she crowed. "I was right. You didn't have to throw yourself at him. You really didn't have to do anything. He likes you. I have to laugh. You thought it was me that he liked, and it's so obviously you."

"Lissa, Lissa," I urged, "you have it all wrong. He never showed the slightest interest in me at the wedding."

"Not at the wedding, silly," Lissa said. "Of course not at the wedding. You're not the same person you were at the wedding."

"Yes, I am."

"You certainly look different."

"That's what you say," I insisted stubbornly. "It isn't true. Looks don't matter anyway. I'm still me on the inside."

She was brushing her hair vigorously, but

she stopped to turn and gaze at me. "Of course you are. But now what you look like gives a better indication of the wonderful person you really are."

"Oh, nonsense," I grumbled. "You're just saying that."

She slapped her brush down on the dresser so hard the mirror shook. When she turned to face me again, her hands were on her hips and her eyes were blazing. "I knocked myself out for you, and you don't even appreciate it. I'd like to shake the stuffing out of you."

"Lissa, please," I begged. "I can explain."

She ignored me. "You were always pretty. Now you're prettier, that's all. A person is pretty if she thinks she's pretty, and you should think you're pretty because you are pretty."

"I think there's a contradiction in there some place," I dared to suggest.

"It may not make sense, but it's true," she insisted. "I'm sick of your attitude, I'll tell you that much. You want to think you're plain. You want to think you look like a little girl. That saves you all the trouble of being nice to guys. You don't have to compete."

I threw myself down on the bed. "If you don't compete, you can't lose," I cried.

"And you can't win either," Lissa snapped. "You should be walking on air. What's the matter with you?"

I stared back at her. What *was* the matter with me? Rory was the most gorgeous guy I'd ever laid eyes on. I was enchanted by him, or at least I had thought I was. He was obviously interested in me. Lissa was right. Of course I should have been walking on air. The foiling of my altruistic plan should not totally obscure from my view the fact that something I had considered totally beyond the realm of possibility was actually happening. Rory Ramussen liked me.

And yet . . . and yet . . . I wasn't walking on air. A stone was sitting in the pit of my stomach, weighing me down. "I thought he was talking to me because he likes to talk," I tried to explain. "I felt bad because you were stuck with Connor all night."

She waved her hand. "Oh, Connor's fun. We have a lot of laughs together. I guess I laughed more tonight than I have in the last two hundred nights put together. I don't mind being with him."

"You don't?" I felt as if the weight in my stomach was going to push me right through the mattress.

Lissa walked over to me and took my hand. "Have fun, Mandy," she said eagerly. "Enjoy yourself. Your dream is coming true. How often in this life does that happen?"

She was right, of course she was right. I made up my mind. The man of my dreams was paying attention to me. His conversation made Connor's and Lissa's talk about cars seem like the brilliant exchanges in eighteenth century French salons, but no one was perfect. He was still gorgeous and kind and generous. And maybe if we could get on another subject, he might even prove amusing.

I fell asleep resolved to do as Lissa said. I fell asleep resolved to have a wonderful time the following day.

Well, I didn't have a *bad* time the following day. It's not possible to have a bad time when the sun is shining, the air is crisp and cold, and you're seated in the Yale Bowl watching the Yale football team clobber Princeton, and white-sweatered cheerleaders are dancing around on the field, and everywhere people are screaming and yelling and jumping up and down, and the guy sitting next to you happens to be the best-looking man in the stadium—and that includes all the players on the field.

And later, at the party, there was plenty of beer to drink and cheese, crackers, potato chips and Fritos to nibble on. Rory sampled only the cheese and one particular whole wheat cracker. Most of the people to whom he introduced us were friendly and warm, with lots to talk about. The party swirled around the college's big living room, and the four of us individually drifted from group to group, rarely talking to the same people at the same time.

After a while I found myself with a nice girl who lived on Rory's floor, her boyfriend, and another guy. I listened while they griped about professors. My eyes searched for my friends. Rory was on the other side of the room, and I couldn't see Lissa at all, which really wasn't surprising since by that time the party had spread all over the college's first floor, and no doubt upstairs too. But after a while I noticed Connor walking toward us.

I got up from the window seat in which I had ensconced myself and headed in his direction. "I haven't seen Rory's room," I said when I reached him. "Let's go up. I want to look at it." Of course I could have asked Rory to show it to me. That would have been more logical. But it was Connor I wanted to talk to.

Connor shot me a quizzical glance but offered no objection. "Follow me," was all he said. He turned, and I threaded my way through the crowd behind him. We climbed two flights of stairs and found ourselves in a long hall. Connor pushed open a door and we entered a pleasant, if rather messy, book-lined room with a large bow window and a fireplace. "This is the study," Connor announced. He plopped himself down into a large floppy red balloon chair. "Six people share it—Rory and his two roommates and the three guys who live in the room on the other side. You want to see Rory's room, just go through there," he added, gesturing toward a door on his right.

"Later," I said, pulling out a desk chair and swinging it around so I could sit facing him. "Right now I want to talk to you. What's the big idea?"

The look of innocence on Connor's face was phony as a three dollar bill. "I don't know what you're talking about. I haven't had a big idea since I decided the yearbook should look like an issue of *Time* magazine."

"We had a deal," I reminded him sternly. "We had an arrangement. You've totally reneged. You haven't done one single thing all weekend to push Lissa and Rory together." I leaned forward and pointed my finger. "It's the bet. You don't want me to win. I should have known you'd be no help under the circumstances." I shook my head and sighed. "I don't understand how I could have been so dumb."

"You're not dumb, kiddo," Connor replied calmly. "One thing you're not is dumb. But you're sure acting dumb. What could I possibly have done to push Lissa and Rory together? It's perfectly obvious to anyone with eyes that the only girl out of the ten thousand females on the Yale campus this weekend in whom Rory has the slightest interest is you."

"If you didn't hang on Lissa like a leech," I retorted, "maybe we could have done something about that."

Connor stubbornly lifted his bearded chin. "I do not hang on to Lissa. She hangs on to me."

"You don't object."

"Why should I object?" Connor shrugged. "You've told me often enough how marvelous Rory is to look at—well, that's just how marvelous to look at I find Lissa. I feel super walking around with her."

"Oh," I replied tightly. "Now I understand."

He stared at me for a long moment. "Do you?" he asked with lifted eyebrows.

"It's an odd match, you and Lissa."

"Now you're talking dumb as well as acting dumb," Connor replied. "It's no match at all. We're thrown together for the weekend and we're enjoying each other's company. That's all there is to that. You don't think a girl who's being pursued by the football captain and the president of the student council at Winter Hill High School will give me a second look once we get back home? You have to understand that this weekend there's simply no one else."

"No one else?" I screamed. "No one else? Forget Rory. Wipe Rory out. There are guys hanging from the rafters in this place. There are guys under the rugs."

"Lissa's not like you," Connor explained. "She's not comfortable with strangers."

"A girl who looks like that?" I retorted. "A girl who draws guys like flies? You're the dumb one."

"You said it yourself."

"I said what myself?"

"At the wedding," Connor reminded me. "You said that there was a kind of shyness to both Lissa and Rory. They're so used to being courted for their appearance that they've never developed the proper social skills."

"That's not exactly what I said," I objected. "It's true of Rory, though," I admitted. "He doesn't have much of an idea of what to talk about with a girl. With anybody, really. I don't think that's true of Lissa, though."

"No," Connor agreed, "it isn't. But she isn't comfortable with a lot of strangers. She's not good at amusing small talk, not like you."

"I'm good at amusing small talk, am I?" I had to laugh. "Tonight is the first time all weekend I've had much of a chance to exercise this skill you're so sure I possess."

"You're the life of the party, Mandy," Connor replied drily.

Suddenly I felt very tired. Perhaps it was the beer. I wasn't really used to drinking beer. If this was how it made me feel, I saw no reason to get used to it. I put my head down on the desk and shut my eyes.

In a moment I felt a hand on my shoulder. I knew it was Connor's hand—whose else could it be? We were the only two people in the suite. I shivered at his touch, and remained motionless for a long moment, letting myself feel the pressure of his warm, firm hand.

Then, suddenly, I wondered what it was I thought I was doing. I opened my eyes and lifted my head to see him standing over me. "You all right, Mandy?" he asked, concern filling his voice and his eyes.

"Sure," I replied. "Just a little tired, that's all."

"But you are having a good time," he said, dropping his hand. "You have to be having a good time. Your dream is coming true."

That's just what Lissa had said the night before. I knew what he meant, but I asked anyway. "What dream?"

"Your dream of Rory." Although he was standing right next to me, his voice sounded as if it were reaching me from a great distance. "That's what this whole game was really about. You had a crush on Rory. Fixing him up with Lissa was just a way to have something to do with him. Now it looks like he has a crush on you too. What could be better—from your point of view, that is," he added.

It was true, of course it was true, and Connor had known it all along. Lissa had known it all along too. Rory was the man of my dreams. And now, as they both had taken such pains to point out, my dream was coming true.

"Under the circumstances," Connor continued sternly, "it's kind of small of you to begrudge Lissa and me a pleasant weekend."

"Yes," I said, much subdued. "You're right. Of course you're right. I'm having a wonderful weekend. I'm glad you're having a nice one too."

"Everything is really working out," he offered heartily. "Isn't it?"

"Oh, yes. Perfectly."

He turned around and moved toward the door. "Perhaps we'd better go back to the party."

"Yes," I agreed. "We'll go back to the party. We'll go back to having a wonderful time." Rigidly I supressed the irony that threatened to invade my voice.

We didn't say much to each other as we went back downstairs. My mind had no room in it for conversation. A litany was ringing in every corner of my brain. "Connor and Lissa. Lissa and Connor. Connor and Lissa. Lissa and Connor." To tell you the truth, I felt absolutely sick. Rory was right about one thing. Too much beer is no good.

A little while later, Connor, Lissa, Rory and I left the party with half a dozen other kids and walked over to a smoky little café where we sat drinking coffee and listening to a young singer trying very hard to convince us he was actually James Taylor. Of course, we didn't all drink coffee. Rory drank herb tea.

That lasted maybe an hour. Then Connor drove Lissa and me back to the hotel. Lissa sat in the front, next to Connor, and Rory sat in the back, next to me. I wasn't fighting it any more. I was riding with the moment. I sat as close to him as I could, and he put his arm around me. He was absolutely gorgeous, and I really did want him to kiss me. I had never kissed a guy, except when we'd played post office and spin-the-bottle in the fifth grade, which didn't count. I had never even gone out with one. And who knew when I'd have another opportunity? Back home, in spite of the new clothes and the new hairdo, nobody was going to kiss me. To them I was still slightly weird Mandy Cobb. In a small town like Winter Hill you don't easily escape the image of yourself, which is usually thoroughly established by the time you're twelve.

But Rory had scarcely known the Mandy Cobb who went to Winter Hill High School. He'd been taken in by the hairdo and the clothes. And he was as gorgeous as any hero of romance. Who could better bestow upon me my very first real kiss? Maybe, if we had the time, more than one kiss. Lissa was right. It was time, finally, to give up dreams and try out the real thing.

But Rory never got any closer to me than that arm around my shoulders. He talked all the way back to the hotel. He had at last exhausted the subject of his health and was now embarked upon a lengthy exposition of his intellectual life. I found out what had transpired in every single class meeting so far that year in his English Comp and Computer courses. If we'd had more time, I soon realized, we wouldn't be spending it making out. He would have seized the opportunity to be equally thorough in his transmittal of information concerning Europe since Napoleon, Basic Chemistry and Advanced German.

Of course I could have kissed him. Such behavior is not unknown in our day and age, and I certainly have no theoretical objection to it. But I couldn't do it. First of all, he didn't stop talking long enough to provide me the opportunity. And second of all, I just didn't have the nerve. Maybe if I'd had a little previous experience, I'd have been able to make the first move. But I don't think so.

Rory was attractive. He was extremely attractive. But he was no make-out artist. I went to bed that night quite as unkissed as I had arisen that morning.

It hadn't been a bad day. Certainly not. But it hadn't been a wonderful day either.

Chapter Eight

MOTHER, Aunt Carrie and Peter were all home when we arrived back in Winter Hill late Sunday afternoon. Lissa had dropped Connor at his house first. "So long, Connor," she said as he climbed out of the car. "It's been a super weekend. Thanks for everything."

"Thank *you*," Connor returned. "I had a great time, too. I'll see you around, Lissa." Then he remembered me. He poked his head over the back seat. "So long, kiddo. See you around."

"Yeah, Connor," I replied. "I guess you will. I have another paper to get out. And I suppose you have another yearbook deadline."

Connor laughed. "I always have another yearbook deadline."

He pulled his body out of the car, picked up his knapsack, and with a wave of his hand and another, "Thanks again, guys," he was gone.

Then, at our house, Lissa and I had to sit at the supper table while the family peppered us with questions. Peter asked about my Saturday morning interview and campus tour. However, those things didn't interest my mother at all.

"But what did you actually *do,* Amanda Jane?" she asked me.

"I'm telling you what I did," I snapped.

"I want to know what you did when you were with Lissa and the boys," my mother explained patiently. She was so eager for information she didn't even call me on my rudeness.

Lissa answered for me, a sly grin spreading over her face. "Mandy did lots of things. Mandy made a conquest."

"How marvelous!" my mother exclaimed. "Who?"

I stared at Lissa, hard, silently reminding her of the pact we had made early that morning, before we'd met the guys for lunch. She got the message. "Someone at Rory's college," she replied airily.

"Do you think you'll see him again?" my mother asked eagerly.

I would surely *see* him again. "I doubt I'll be going out with him," I replied carefully. "It was just a weekend thing. We had some fun, that's all."

"Well, that's all right," my mother said. She

didn't even sound too disappointed. "It's good experience."

I escaped from the dinner table as soon as I could, pleading the pressure of all the homework I'd left undone so far that weekend. It was a legitimate excuse. I was at my desk struggling with the mysteries of analytical geometry when Lissa knocked at my door and then entered without waiting for my reply.

"Mandy," she said, plopping down on my bed, "I have to talk to you."

I looked up at her. Even sprawled on my bed she looked graceful and perfectly groomed. "So talk."

"I want you to let me out of my promise not to tell the folks that you and Rory are. . . ." She hesitated for a moment, searching for the right phrase.

"Are what?"

"You know," she said. "A thing."

"We're not a thing," I banged my fist on my desk. "He didn't even kiss me."

"He's shy," Lissa said. "He will, next time."

"We agreed, Lissa," I insisted. "We agreed it would be just too complicated and embarrassing to say anything, with Rory's father living right in this house. I couldn't face him at breakfast and dinner every day. I just couldn't."

"I think you're silly."

"Well, it's me, Lissa, that's all," I replied, with a violent shake of my head. "You have to respect my wishes in this case."

"But Rory will be home for Thanksgiving. You know he's going to ask you out. What'll we do then?"

"Let's wait until it happens before we do anything," I temporized. "Because I don't think it will happen. He didn't even kiss me."

"You said that before," Lissa replied with a shrug. "What does that mean? Why are you so hung up on kisses all of a sudden?"

"Frankly, Lissa," I deigned to explain, "it isn't an awful lot of fun to talk to Rory, and in the dark you can't look at him. I thought he might be good for kissing."

Lissa giggled. "When you find out, let me know."

That was a surprising remark. It made me think of something else. "Listen, there's something I want to ask you." I rushed to get the words out before I lost my nerve. "Did you ever start things up with a boy? I mean, did you ever make the first move?"

She grinned. "Well, you let them know you're interested. Sit close, touch them accidentally on purpose, you know, that sort of thing."

"Did you ever kiss first?"

Lissa shook her head. "I don't think I ever wanted to."

"I don't think you ever had to," I returned sadly. "I tried all the other stuff."

"I told you. He's shy," she repeated.

"A Yale freshman and shy. What's he been doing all these years?"

"Making something out of himself," Lissa retorted. "Really, you have to admire him."

"Admire him? Why?"

"Four years ago, Rory was a joke. Look at him now. He did it all by himself. Well, Coach Samber over at Brookville High helped him, but mainly he did it by himself. The first time I met Rory was when Peter took Mom and me to watch him run a cross-country race. Do you remember?"

"Vaguely." It had happened the previous spring. "What could be more boring than watching a cross-country race? Mostly you see country, not race."

"We came for the end and stood at the finish line, so it wasn't too bad," Lissa explained. "Afterwards, Peter told us all about how Rory had built himself up. Saved himself, Peter said."

"You mean he was so weak he might have died?"

"No, silly, not die physically. But sort of die inside, if you know what I mean."

"Psychologically," I suggested. "Emotionally."

Lissa nodded. "And now, it's not only his own body he's concerned about. He wants other people to be healthy too."

"Yeah, like with the Coke," I remembered. "Really, he could drive a person crazy."

"You know, Mandy," Lissa scolded, "I think that's basically an unkind remark. Rory is very different from most other health nuts. They're totally selfish. But Rory volunteers in a drug rehab program in New Haven. He teaches kids body building and nutrition."

"He never told me about that." The good stuff was what he neglected to mention.

"He never told me either. He told Peter, and Peter told Mom, and Mom told me."

"Well, you never told me about it."

"You and I were in a different place three months ago, when he started. I wasn't telling you much of anything then. And last spring, I tried to ignore Rory's very existence. To have done anything else would have been to admit to myself that Mother and Peter were on their way to the altar. I managed to avoid most of the little outings Mom or Peter planned for the four of us."

She uttered a small ironic laugh. "Much good it did me. And maybe it was a mistake. Maybe I should have gotten to know Rory better. I don't think I could have, though. He begged off as often as I did. I think I saw him maybe four times before the wedding. I guess he wasn't any more eager to be my brother than I was to be his sister. I don't blame him for that."

"He talks too much," I complained.

"To you," Lissa said. "The few times I saw him with Mom and Peter, he barely opened his mouth."

"Look, Lissa," I reminded her, "you just said you don't know him very well yourself. I may know him better, and I don't think I'll be going out with Rory when he comes home for Thanksgiving. So let's not get started with Peter and my mother and all of that. OK? If he does ask me out, then we can explain. But you know my mother. If nothing comes of it, she'll die of disappointment. Please, Lissa?"

"All right." Lissa's tone was resigned. "I promised, and I'll keep my promise, even though I don't agree with you. I just know he's going to ask you out. Then they'll really be mad at us for not having told them anything sooner."

"I'll take care of it. I'll think of something."

A frown momentarily creased the perfect smoothness of Lissa's forehead. "You're always thinking of something. One day you'll get into trouble that way."

I already had. But I didn't tell her that. She left then, to do her own homework. I stayed up late, finishing mine. Finally I got into bed and picked up my book.

———

"... So good you were! So—so kind! But you don't want to marry me, Alverstoke. You know you don't!"

"Of course I don't," he responded with great cordiality. "But since two of my sisters, my secretary—damn his impudence!—and at least two of my oldest friends, are apparently convinced, in spite of all my efforts to throw dust in their eyes, that that is my ambition, I do beg of you, Frederica, to accept my offer! I cannot—I really cannot endure the mortification of being rejected!"

... She said unsteadily: "You are all goodness—all kindness! I don't know—I am not sure—why you have made me this offer: whether because you think you compromised me, or, perhaps—out of compassion, which is quite misplaced, but which I fancy you have sometimes felt, but—"

———

"Really, Frederica, you should know better than to talk such twaddle!" he expostulated. "Of all the moonshine—! I am neither good nor kind. I did not compromise you: and if I thought you an object for my compassion I should also think you a dead bore, my girl! But you have never bored me." He possessed himself of her hands and held them firmly. . . .

She was trembling, her brain in a whirl. "Oh, impossible! You are not—in love with me! How could you be? Are you trying to—to hoax me into believing that? No, no, don't!"

"Oh, not in the least!" he assured her cheerfully. "It is merely that I find I cannot live without you, my adorable Frederica!"

———————

I tossed the book aside. I didn't feel much like reading after all. In the books the heroes were not only handsome; they were usually witty and charming besides. Sometimes the charm was dark and mysterious, even threatening, but it was there. In real life, the man who looks like the hero of your fantasies can turn out to be about as interesting as a dish of turnips.

And the charming one, the witty one, the one who's a lot of fun—you may not even have noticed him until it was too late.

———————

I sat up in bed with a start. Was that it? Was Rory Ramussen the man of my dreams? Or was he really Connor Borne? Skinny, hollow-cheeked, acned Connor Borne?

Clever, affectionate, red-bearded Connor Borne. Connor Borne, who'd been a friendly acquaintance nearly all my life, and now was truly a friend. Connor Borne, who called me "kiddo," and borrowed my paste pot, and made silly bets with me and wouldn't even tell me what they were. Connor Borne, who, I was suddenly able to admit to myself, lifted my heart when he touched me, with his eyes, or his hand. And who threw me into a jealous fit when he turned those eyes and hands to Lissa. That's why a kind of pall had descended upon me during the weekend. I'd been jealous. Jealous of Connor and Lissa.

What an idiot I had been. And now it was too late. I might be seeing Connor in a new way, but to him I was still the same little old Mandy Cobb I'd always been. He would never be able to see me any differently than he always had.

And who could blame him? After all, when had the scales been lifted from my eyes? Not until this weekend. Not until we were all up at Yale, in a new place, where we'd never been before. Not until I'd suddenly noticed his red head and

Lissa's honey-colored one leaning close together, their faces full of laughter, their words to each other too swift and low for me to quite make out.

There was nothing to be done about it now. A new hairdo and new clothes certainly didn't make me any competition for Lissa—except maybe in Rory's eyes, for reasons I didn't entirely understand. When we'd entered the restaurant Friday evening, he had looked at Lissa first, greeted Lissa first. I had thought, for just a minute or two, that Rory had been a lot more affected by Connor's letter than he had admitted in his reply. But then the Coke had spilled, and I realized that I had been mistaken.

Now I knew that Rory really couldn't see Lissa, and Lissa really couldn't see Rory. Her mother and his father were married to each other. That fact stood irrevocably in their way. Romantically excited by my own manipulations, I had refused to acknowledge the obstacle. But now I had to admit to it. Rory was the only man in the world who could see me and Lissa standing next to each other and pick me.

It was ironic really. Thinking it was Rory I loved, I had in a grand gesture of self-sacrifice sought to fix him up with Lissa. But it had turned out to be no such grand gesture after all. It was actually a very easy thing to do because it wasn't really Rory I cared about. It was Connor. And realizing that Connor and Lissa *really* liked each other did not fill me with feelings of noble altruism. It filled me with feelings of shameful envy.

What a muddle. I was sorry I had ever gotten involved with men of real flesh and blood. My life had been a lot less painful when my only romances were in books. Trilby, come back, come back, I cried to myself. I need you now.

But I feared that a cat would never be enough for me again. You cannot kiss a cat. Well, you can, but it's not the same thing. Of course, to be perfectly honest, I still didn't know that for sure. And the way things looked now, it could be years, literally years, before I did. If ever.

Still, during the ensuing weeks, at least on schooldays, I was not nearly so actively miserable as I'd expected to be that Sunday night as I lay restless and discontented in my bed. I was all by myself, but for a while it didn't seem to matter. Just as Connor had predicted, Lissa returned to Willie Travertine and Stan Schneiderman and Iggie Rowson and Rob Palowski, and Connor returned to his schoolwork and his job at McDonalds and the yearbook, and I returned to my schoolwork and my novels and the newspaper.

Connor and I hung out in the publications room and laughed and joked with each other, just as we always had. Nothing had changed. At least not to look at.

The Saturday night before Thanksgiving I was sitting in the back parlor wrapped in a quilt against the chill. Victorian houses are wonderful in spring, summer and early fall, but in cold weather it requires stamina to live in them.

I was watching "Saturday Night Live." Not one single skit struck me as even slightly funny. I was absolutely alone in the house and once again feeling extremely cross. I had been alone a hundred other Saturday nights and not minded it, at least not very much. But that night I wished I were out somewhere, with Connor, or even with Rory, out anywhere, laughing and flirting and having fun. One weekend in New Haven, a highly problematic weekend at that, and already I was spoiled.

I heard the front door slam. A moment later Lissa entered the room and plopped down on the couch.

"You're home early," I commented.

"I told Willie I had a headache." She sounded as cross as I felt.

"I'll get you some aspirin," I offered.

"I don't really have a headache, dummy."

"Oh." I was silent, waiting for her to tell me more, if she wanted to.

"I'm sick of Willie Travertine and his big, dirty hands roaming all over the place."

"Imagine, the president of the student council having dirty hands. Maybe I ought to write an article about that. A big exposé."

Lissa smiled, but it was a smile without any enthusiasm. "The president of the student council is a nerd," she said.

"How about the captain of the football team?"

"Stan Schneiderman is also a nerd." Her voice suggested that was her final word on the subject. She sighed. "It's all so boring, so awfully boring."

"I should be so bored," I commented drily. "Try spending a Saturday night in front of the idiot box."

"I may, next week," she said. "They both asked me to the Charity Ball."

"Which one are you going with? Or will Rob or Iggie win the precious prize?"

"Don't be sarcastic, Mandy," she protested.

"I didn't mean to be," I returned seriously. "You *are* the prize—the prize of the Winter Hill High School senior class."

The glance she shot me had a question in it.

"What would you say if I went to the Charity Ball with Connor?"

"He asked you?" I was surprised. I had been lulled, the previous two weeks, into believing he really didn't have the nerve to pursue a relationship with Lissa.

She shook her head. "No, but it won't be hard to see to it that he does."

"I never thought of Connor as your type." I forced my voice to sound mild and disinterested.

"I know," she replied dreamily. "But we had so much fun at Yale. We laughed and laughed. That's what matters, you know—not how famous a guy is."

"You don't say." Now I was being sarcastic.

She didn't seem to hear me. "Of course, I could never be in love with Connor. But you don't have to be in love with a guy to go with him to the Charity Ball. I've been to three Charity Balls, and the only time I was with a guy I really liked was last year, when I went with Howie."

"Too bad he moved away." My words were more heartfelt than she could know.

"Well, there's no point in mourning over that anymore," she announced briskly. "I've shed enough tears for Howie Pridman, the rat. You know what, Mandy?"

"What, Lissa?"

"With his beard, Connor isn't so bad looking. Have you noticed that?"

"I can't say that I have," I lied.

"But I won't let him kiss me," she added with finality. "The beard would scratch."

I could think of nothing I'd like better than to be scratched by Connor's beard. But I certainly wasn't going to enter the lists against Lissa. I had done some pretty dumb things in the past couple of months, but that dumb I wasn't. As Lissa herself had pointed out, I didn't like entering contests I had no chance of winning. All I said was, "Is that really fair, Lissa? I mean to make Connor go to the ball with you, and then not even kiss him?"

She stared at me. "You shock me, Mandy," she said. "I won't *make* Connor take me to the ball. He wants to. He just doesn't have the nerve to ask me, that's all."

"I'm sure he wants to kiss you too," I said.

"Well, if he works up the guts to do that, I guess I can't stop him," she said. "But I won't encourage it."

It really wasn't fair. It wasn't fair at all. Lissa had everything under such perfect control. The affection I'd felt for her since just before the wedding was evaporating. My old jealousy and discomfort in her presence were rapidly returning. I was mad at myself for that. She'd done nothing to deserve my dislike. She'd been wonderful to me for weeks now. She couldn't know how I felt about Connor. Why, I hardly knew how I felt about him myself. My feelings may have lain dormant deep inside me for a long time, but they were very newly hatched, barely formed. I ought to be able to do the sensible thing and exorcise them.

I stood up. "All this TV is no good for me," I said. "Now I'm getting a headache. A real one. I'm going to bed." That seemed by far the best thing to do. It was easier to remember my obligations to Lissa when I wasn't in the same room with her.

Lissa stood up. "Me too," she said.

I snapped off the TV. She turned out the lights and started up the stairs. I trailed behind her. We said very little. When we reached the third floor hallway, she turned to me. "Good night, Mandy," she said.

"Good night, Lissa," I replied. She walked into her room and shut the door behind her. I went into the bathroom. It was freezing cold in there. Heat's supposed to rise, but when the pipes are old, it's asking too much of it to expect it to make its way all the way to the third floor, especially since Peter and my father were so enthusiastic about saving energy that they wouldn't allow us to push the thermostat above sixty-five degrees during the day or fifty-five at night. Quickly I popped two aspirin into my mouth, swallowed them with water, and then brushed my teeth. I didn't bother with anything else. I was already wearing my flannel nightshirt. I leaped into bed, pulled the warm quilt up over my head and lay perfectly still curled up in the fetal position, so as not to touch the cold parts of the sheets. In a few minutes, I was warm again, and then I was able to fall asleep.

Chapter Nine

 THURSDAY was Thanksgiving. In the morning Lissa and I went to the traditional football game, Winter Hill *vs.* Brookville. We didn't go together. She went with Rob and Iggie; I went with two other girls. Everyone was there, of course. At the refreshment stand during half time, Winter Hill leading seven to nothing, I encountered Rory. I had known he would be there. He was a graduate of Brookville High. But I had not counted on running into him.

When he saw me, he called out, "Mandy! What luck to find you in this mob. I was going to call you." He was at my side in three long strides, his hand grasping my upper arm. "What luck," he repeated.

"Hi, Rory. How are you?"

"Fine, great. What do you want? I'll get it for you. You'll never be able to push your way to the counter through this crowd."

"I'm cold," I said. "I want some hot chocolate."

"All that sugar?" he queried, a disapproving frown creasing his forehead.

"Rory, they don't have anything healthy here. It's either hot chocolate or coffee, and I prefer the chocolate."

"Well," he responded grudgingly, "of the two I guess that's the better choice. Wait over by the fence."

I obeyed him. In a few minutes he was back with two steaming cups. He sipped his own with apparent relish. "I have to have dinner with my mother," he said. "but after that I'll drive over to say hello to my dad. Then maybe you and I can go to the movies or something."

So it hadn't been a weekend thing. Rory did intend to pursue the relationship now that he was home again. How did I feel about that? I wasn't exactly sure. But something told me Rory was better than nothing. A lot better.

"OK," I said, trying to strike exactly the right note: interested but not wildly enthusiastic.

"Maybe Lissa and Connor will come with us too," he said. Clearly, he considered them a thing.

"Lissa probably already has a date. With Rob or Iggie," I added, to make sure he understood. So far as I knew, she had not yet informed Connor of the fact that his was to be the inestimable honor of escorting her to the Charity Ball.

"Well, check it out, will you?" Rory asked.

I looked him straight in the eye. "No, Rory," I said, "I don't think I can do that."

"Oh, OK, then," Rory said. "We'll let it go." But he sounded a little disappointed. What did he need Lissa and Connor for, I wondered. Protection?

And then, in the end, he didn't let it go. It turned out that Lissa did not have a date that night. Rory found that out almost as soon as he got to our house. My mother played right into his hands. "The four of us are going over to the Van Nests' this evening," she said, her voice, as always, gentle and eminently persuasive. "You young people ought to do something together."

Rory smiled. "That's what we are planning. You busy, Lissa?"

She shook her head.

"You're not?" I guess my amazement was written all over my face.

"I told Rob and Iggie all I'd want to do after consuming our monster turkey was sleep," she replied casually. "But that was earlier. Now dinner's over, and I'm bored. I'd like to go to the movies with you guys." She looked at me, her brows raised. Her eyes were saying, "Unless you want to be alone with Rory."

Since I didn't know what I wanted, I replied enthusiastically, "Great. That'll be just great."

My mother looked from me to Rory and then back at me again. From the expression in her eyes I could tell that a light bulb had gone on inside her head. She turned to Aunt Carrie, her expression conveying a message to her sister.

Then of course Rory had to say, "Maybe Connor would like to come, too."

"Maybe he would," Lissa said with a smile. "Why don't you call him up and ask him?" Which Rory did, immediately, and naturally Connor said he'd be delighted to join us. So now Connor had a date with Lissa right at home in Winter Hill and he hadn't even had to suffer the anticipation of a possible rejection, which he would have experienced if he had to think about asking her out himself.

I was annoyed, to say the least, but at the same time I wasn't blind to the humor of the situation. Only it would have seemed a lot funnier if someone other than me had been cast in the part of the fool. I had intended to play go-between for Rory and Lissa. Instead, Rory was playing go-between for Connor and Lissa. It would have been a great joke if it hadn't been on me.

We went to the movies. That's one of three things to do at night in Winter Hill. Rory sat with his arm around me, as he had in the car in New Haven. Connor's arm was not around Lissa, but he could have been holding her hand. I wasn't sure. It was too dark for me to see.

Afterwards, at the diner where we went for something to eat, I did my very best to see to it that the conversation remained general among the four of us. We talked about the game and school and kids we knew. But when we got into the car, Lissa said, "I'm not sleepy. Let's not go right home. Let's cruise around a little." It was Rory's car so he, of course, was driving. I sat in front with him, and Lissa and Connor were in the back.

"I'll drive up to Rebel's Point," Rory said, "and we can look at the view."

At night, the view from Rebel's Point was lovely. You could see necklaces of lights sparkling across the whole valley, which was stretched out below the hill like a patchwork quilt. But if we actually parked at Rebel's Point and actually just looked at the view, we'd be the first people who'd ever done that. The Point was the most notorious make-out spot in the county.

However, we looked at the view. We actually just looked at the view.

The four of us got out of the car and stood at the edge of a shale outcropping, gazing down at Winter Hill and Brookville and half a dozen other little towns marked out before us as clearly as on a map. For a moment we were silent.

But then Connor spoke. "Isn't there a rock around here or something? I want to sit down."

"Most kids when they come up here," Lissa replied with a light laugh, "don't even get out of their cars."

"Come on, Connor," Rory said. "We'll get a rock." He moved off to the parking lot, which was lined with large whitewashed boulders. "We'll take one of these."

Connor followed, complaining. "What're you, nuts or something, Rory?"

Rory pointed to the nearest one. "OK, Connor, grab one end, I'll grab the other, and we'll heave."

"You want me to get a hernia? I can sit in the car."

"In the car you can hardly see the view at all," Rory insisted. He put his hands under the rock and lifted it two-thirds of the way off the ground. "You won't have to do much—just provide balance."

"My God," Lissa whispered, "he's turned himself into a regular Mr. America. It's amazing! It's wonderful!"

"You do have to give him credit," I admitted.

A few moments later, Rory and Connor settled the rock along the shale outcropping. Connor was panting and groaning; I don't think Rory was even sweating.

But the rock was only big enough for two. "You guys take it," Lissa said. "I'm cold anyway. Connor and I will wait in the car."

"My sentiments exactly," Connor responded. The two of them hurried back toward the parking lot. Rory sat down on the rock and patted the space next to him.

"I'm cold too," I said. Remembering Lissa's suggestions, I arranged myself as close to him as I could get.

He put his arm around me, but he made no attempt to kiss me. He talked and talked. I listened and listened. He said I was the most understanding person he'd ever met. He said I was the first one who cared about his ideas. I didn't tell him he was jumping to conclusions.

Lissa and Connor remained in the car. It was much too dark and they were too far away for me to have any idea of what they were doing. It was a good thing I couldn't see them. If I could have, I'd have been tempted to look, and I didn't relish the idea of turning into a Peeping Tom.

Even our house seemed cozy with welcoming warmth after half an hour perched in the wind on top of a mountain. After we said good night to the guys and entered the front hall, Lissa and I realized that Mother, Dad, Carrie and Peter were already in bed. Thank goodness their inquisition would be delayed until morning. But there were a few things I wanted to say to Lissa. I followed her into her bedroom uninvited. I pulled the afghan from the end of her bed and wrapped myself in it while I sat in her armchair watching her undress and carefully put each item of clothing away before she removed the next one.

"Aren't you cold?" I asked.

"No," she replied, standing there in her bra while she neatly folded her sweater.

"But you said you were cold before, at Rebel's Point. You sure were in a hurry to get back into the car."

She whirled around. "What are you asking me? Are you asking me if Connor and I made out?"

"Yeah," I mumbled, picking at my cuticle.

"Well, we didn't," she said. "I mean, he put his arm around me, but that's all. I told you, I'm not interested in him in that way. And he's not very experienced, you know. He doesn't make any moves."

I felt like a condemned criminal who's been reprieved. But I knew it was only for the moment. How long would Connor's inexperience act as a restraint? He was normal, after all. What would happen after the Charity Ball, when they'd been dancing together all evening?

"What about you?" she asked. "What were you and Rory doing on that rock all that time?"

"Not a damn thing." I sighed. I supposed Rory was normal too. At least, he appeared normal. And he certainly seemed to want something from me. Only that something apparently had virtually nothing to do with the fact that I was a girl and he was a guy. Maybe he hadn't noticed.

In the morning when my mother quizzed me, I wished I could say that to her. But of course I couldn't. Peter was there too, at the breakfast table, grinning like a Cheshire cat. "It was Rory, wasn't it?" my mother said. "He was your conquest that weekend at Yale."

"I think conquest is the wrong word, Mother," I replied as calmly as I could. "We just went around together, that's all. The four of us went around together."

"It didn't look like nothing yesterday." Peter felt obliged to stick in his two cents. "Rory hardly swallowed his turkey at his mother's house before he rushed over here. I certainly wasn't the attraction."

"What I can't understand," Carrie said, turning to Lissa, "is why you didn't tell us it was Rory right off. Why all the secrecy?"

"Why? Why?" my father chimed in. Thank goodness for my father. "Can't you see why? The poor girl's face is the color of a ripe tomato. It can't be easy to be involved with someone who's more or less a member of the family. You get the feeling that your private life is being carried on in a fishbowl."

Gratefully I put my hand on his arm. "Thanks, Dad," I murmured. Then I added more strongly, "But there's nothing going on. Nothing that we couldn't do with perfect comfort in a fishbowl." I turned and looked hard at my mother. Then I awarded Peter a similar stare. "Do you understand?"

"Sure, sure." Peter nodded, not believing a word I was saying.

"I wish you were a smidge more confiding,

Amanda Jane," my mother announced sadly. I knew she longed for comfortable private chats in her bedroom between the two of us about clothes and men. Finally I had a beau and I refused to talk about him. Naturally she was disappointed. But that's how she was going to have to stay. Anyway, I had told the truth. There was nothing to chat about.

"Maybe if it were someone else," my father said. "But surely, Mary Belle, under the circumstances you can understand Mandy's reticence."

So I was off the hook. For a while.

Friday night the four of us went bowling. Drinking was the second thing you could do at night in Winter Hill after the movies. Bowling was the third.

Saturday night Rory and his father and Carrie drove to the city for a hockey game. Rory asked Peter to try to get a ticket for me too, but the Garden was all sold out. My parents were also out. Connor came over after work. He, Lissa and I spent the rest of the evening in our back parlor watching TV and eating homemade popcorn. "Saturday Night Live" seemed much much funnier with company than it had when I was alone. The three of us sat on the sofa, Connor ensconced between Lissa and me.

He put his arms around both of us. "Every guy in Winter Hill would envy me if they could see me now," he said with a laugh. "Here I am with the two best-looking girls in town and no competition."

The touch of Connor's hand on my shoulder sent an electric shiver down my spine. I picked up the empty bowl from the coffee table. "I'll get some more popcorn," I said. But I came back quickly. I was uncomfortable when I was with them; at the same time I didn't want to let them out of my sight.

But when I returned they were no closer together than they had been when I left. And after I put the bowl of popcorn back down on the table, Connor took his arm from Lissa's shoulder and began eating. So everything was all right again, for a while. Neither Connor nor Lissa made any attempt to get rid of me. And they could have gone out if they had wanted to. Connor had his father's car. Instead Connor left in the middle of the late movie, and Lissa and I didn't finish watching it. We just went to bed.

I didn't see Rory on Sunday. He spent the morning with his mother and left for New Haven in the afternoon. But he called. First he talked with his father. Then he asked to speak to me.

"Listen, Mandy," he said, "I just called to say goodbye."

"Well, goodbye, Rory. Good luck on your exams."

"I'll see you before exams. I'll be back in two weeks. For the Charity Ball. Will you go with me?"

The Charity Ball. It was the biggest social event of the year in Winter Hill. The Winter Hill Hospital Auxiliary ran it. They had been running it for centuries. It kept right on going, through depression, through war, through social revolution. Clothes changed, manners changed, music changed, values changed, but the Charity Ball had outlasted many elaborate, world-famous affairs. It was like nothing else I'd ever heard of. It was held at the country club, dress was formal, and all the grown-ups went, and all the kids went too. At the age of ten in Winter Hill, you started wondering who would take you to your first Charity Ball, and when. I, of course, had never been asked before. But I certainly wanted to go. It was the only event in Winter Hill that bore even the faintest resemblance to the assemblies and dances described so glowingly in the Regency romances and Gothic novels I loved.

"Yes, Rory," I replied. "I'll go with you."

"Swell," he said. "I'll see you then. We'll double with Connor and Lissa."

"Swell," I echoed. If there was any irony in my response, he didn't catch it.

"See you soon."

"Yes. Goodbye, Rory." I replaced the receiver and went to look for my mother. I had to tell her right away I needed a dress. It certainly would be difficult now that I was going to the Charity Ball with Rory to maintain my claim that there was really nothing of importance between us. But everything has its price. And I did want to go to the ball. I did. I really did.

I went upstairs to find Lissa. She was in her room, sewing patches on old jeans. I didn't know why. She'd never wear them.

"Well," I said, plopping down on her bed, "Rory asked me to the Charity Ball. We're going to double with you and Connor, if that's all right."

"All right? All right!" Lissa exclaimed. "It's wonderful. It's terrific. I'm so happy. I'm thrilled, to tell you the truth." She sounded a hundred times more excited than I was.

She laid down her sewing, rose from her chair and came to sit next to me on the bed. "It all worked out," she said. "It worked out just the way we'd hoped and planned."

"Not the way I'd hoped and planned," I murmured.

"Well, maybe not the way you'd planned," Lissa responded smiling, "but certainly the way you'd hoped. Anyway, by 'we' I didn't mean you and me. I meant me and Connor."

"You and Connor?" I drew back, not understanding. "What do you and Connor have to do with Rory and me?"

She laughed. "We cooked up a little scheme between us. I knew you liked Rory from the day of Mom's wedding, and I asked Connor to help me get the two of you together, and he said he would."

I swallowed hard. "Did you have a bet?"

"A bet? What do you mean, a bet? What kind of bet?"

"I don't know," I replied darkly. "Connor appears to be a gambling man." Also a stinker, a rat and louse. But I didn't say that part out loud.

I didn't see Connor on Monday or Tuesday. Wednesday the paper had a staff meeting. Connor was seated quietly at a table on the opposite side of the room, working. I waited until the meeting was over, amazed at my own self-control. When most of the others had left, I walked over to him.

"OK, Connor," I said very quietly. "You won."

He looked up from the proof pages spread out before him. "Won what?"

"The bet."

"The bet?" His expression was blank.

"Don't pretend you don't know what I'm talking about. Rory and Lissa. They're not going to the Charity Ball together. So you won."

"Oh, yes, the bet." His eyes returned to his proof pages.

I put my hand down on top of them and bent my face into his. "Well, what did you win? I want to know what I owe you."

He withdrew his hand from under mine and pushed back his chair. "We weren't supposed to open the envelope until after the Charity Ball, kiddo," he said. "Remember?"

"I remember." I spit out each word. "But do you remember? You made an arrangement with me. Then you went and made the same arrangement with Lissa. You're a piece of work, Connor Borne. You're a double-crosser and a louse. Now I understand why you were so totally unhelpful.

I thought it was just because you wanted to win the bet. There was a lot more to it than that."

"Lissa says I didn't help her very much either." There was a crack in his voice as he spoke. "So what difference did it make in the end? I just told Lissa I'd go along with her because I realized . . . well, I realized it was what you really wanted."

"What was it I really wanted, Connor?" I snapped. "You tell me."

"Rory," he murmured. "You wanted Rory." His voice grew stronger and angrier. "Well, now you're going to the ball with him. Lissa told me. You didn't. And we're supposed to be friends."

"What did you expect me to do? Report the news as soon as Rory and I had hung up the phone?" I felt the tears well up in the back of my eyes, and I blinked hard three times to force them to retreat. "We're not friends, Connor. Not after the way you've acted."

He shook his head and sighed. "I don't understand, Mandy. I don't understand. You have what you want."

"And you have what you want," I retorted. "You have Lissa."

"Is that what you think, Mandy?" His voice

was so quiet I had to lean forward to hear him. "I don't have Lissa. We're going to the ball together, that's all. It's convenient for her. She didn't have to make a choice among any of the serious contenders. As for me, I'm flattered. OK? What's wrong with that? Just the way you are when you're seen with Rory."

I clenched my fists together. I had thought he understood me. He understood nothing. But then how could he? I had never given him the slightest hint that I had changed direction so completely. I was glad now that I hadn't. I couldn't trust him. I didn't want to have anything to do with him. "I'll double with you for the ball, Connor," I said, "because I don't see how I could explain all of this to Lissa and Rory. But after that, I don't care if I ever lay eyes on you again."

There was nothing else for me to say—or to hear. I turned around and rushed out of the room. I couldn't force the tears back any longer, and I certainly wasn't going to let him see them. I pushed them away with my fist, like a six year old. I wasn't going to cry over Connor. I wasn't. He was beyond my comprehension.

Chapter Ten

 SATURDAY Lissa and I went shopping together for the third time in our lives. This time was the best. This time someone else wasn't dressing me up like a doll. Instead, Lissa and I embarked upon a joint expedition, equally beneficial to each of us.

We didn't find anything in Winter Hill and drove on to two different shopping centers. By day's end, we were exhausted but satisfied. Even me. Lissa had purchased a gown of sea green chiffon with a low cut, close-fitting bodice held up by spaghetti straps, and a three-tiered skirt that whirled when she moved. She was tall enough to carry it off.

My dress was of a clinging burgundy fabric that made more of my every curve than was actually there. With its long sleeves and deeply plunging V neckline, it couldn't have been simpler, but the mirror told me it became me as no other garment I'd ever owned. For once I was satisfied with my appearance. I was sure my mother would lend me her antique gold and garnet pin to wear with the gown. I'd look twenty-two years old and frightfully sophisticated. Maybe Rory would notice. Maybe the night of the ball he'd do something instead of just talk, talk, talk. I was so pleased with my appearance I actually began to look forward to going. Rory and I would dance every dance. We'd spend virtually no time whatsoever with Lissa and Connor. Maybe I could find a third couple to go along with us. The more people between me and Connor, the better.

Connor didn't come over that Saturday night. He had to work. They were shorthanded at McDonalds. Two guys had quit, and he had to cover until they hired more help. "I'm rich," he told Lissa, "but exhausted."

Lissa went out with Stan Schneiderman. "That's shocking," I said to my mother. "Stan should be going out with Phyllis Esposito tonight. He's taking her to the ball, and you're supposed to pay some attention to your date for the ball the week before it comes off. I mean, you're supposed to be going with someone you like, for heaven's sake."

"It was different when I was young," my mother said with a sigh. "When I was young, a girl could go out with one boy Friday night and a different one on Saturday. And vice versa, for that matter. At a party, the idea was to dance with as many different boys as possible.

We were in the kitchen, fixing some cocoa and cookies to carry into the back parlor, where we'd been watching TV with Peter and Carrie. My father was out of town, for a change. "I don't know as I approve of this modern style of one at a time," my mother continued. "That can get heavy. I think Lissa has the right idea. If you play the field, you don't get involved too deeply before you know how to handle it."

That was an interesting theory. I had never thought of that before. I had just assumed Lissa was merely fickle—and lucky. But maybe in her own way she was just as scared as on two different occasions she had accused me of being.

"Someone's at the back door," my mother said. Her face wore a listening look.

"I don't hear a thing," I said.

But then a firm set of knuckles rapped sharply against the wooden panel. Someone was there, and whoever it was had realized that the back doorbell was broken. "I'll get it, Amanda," my mother said. "I wonder who it could be at this hour?" She switched on the outside light, pulled aside the curtain that covered the little window in the upper part of the door and peered out. "It's Connor," she said. "Connor Borne."

"Maybe he doesn't know Lissa went out to-night," I said. "Don't tell him about Stan." The words were out of my mouth before I realized what I was saying. Why on earth was I trying to protect Connor's feelings? Hadn't I told myself ten dozen times I was through caring about Connor?

"Come in, Connor," my mother said as she opened the door. "I'm sorry, but Lissa isn't here."

"That's OK, Mrs. Cobb," Connor said as he entered the kitchen. "I didn't come to see Lissa." He looked oddly misshapen. For some reason, one of his jacket sleeves hung empty, and he was holding his arm under his coat.

"What's the matter, Connor?" I wondered. "Did you break your arm?"

"Not yet," he replied. With his free hand he reached inside his jacket and pulled out a scrawny, shivering half-grown tricolored cat.

"Oh, Connor, where did you dig up such a forlorn-looking creature!" my mother ex-claimed. "And why ever did you bring it here?"

"It belongs to Mandy. Doesn't it, Mandy?"

I took the pitiful thing from his hands and cradled her in my arms. "It could be," I said. "It certainly could be." I could feel her ribs beneath her scruffy fur. Without putting her down, I poured some milk into a saucepan to heat up on the stove.

"What could be?" My mother was clearly mystified.

"I found this cat out by the garbage back of McDonalds," Connor explained. "I think it's Mandy's."

"Mandy's?" My mother remained unenlightened.

It was my turn. "Remember the cats that lived up in the loft until the weather turned cold? This could be one of the kittens. I'm almost sure that she is. Of course, she's lost a lot of weight, but the coloring is right." I set her down and put the milk in a bowl on the floor. She lapped at it eagerly, but neatly, like a lady, even though I could tell by looking at her that she was starving. "See? She eats just the way Trilby ate. I'm sure she's Trilby's daughter."

"Yes, I thought so," Connor said.

"And you don't even like cats," I reminded him.

"You don't have to like cats to recognize them," he retorted.

"I don't like cats either," my mother said.

"Oh, Mom," I moaned, "you're not going to make me put her out in the cold now, are you? After all she's gone through? After all the losses that she's suffered? I mean, where's her mother? Where are her brothers and sisters?"

"You keep saying 'she' and 'her,' " my mother commented. "How do you know?"

"Tricolors are always females," Connor interjected. "It's a sex-linked characteristic. Appropriate, don't you think?"

I didn't know whether that was a compliment or an insult, and with my mother's next remark I realized I didn't have time to find out. "Male or female," she said, "the creature can't stay here."

"But it's too cold in the loft. That's why they left in the first place," I pointed out, desperation sending my voice up two octaves.

But my mother shook her head.

"You know, Mrs. Cobb," Connor announced, "cats are very clean. You just put some sand in a box and they use that automatically."

My mother didn't say anything.

Encouraged, Connor continued. "I'm sure if you left her in that utility room you have off the kitchen, she wouldn't bother anyone."

"Yeah, Mom," I added quickly. "I'd take

such good care of her, you wouldn't even know she was there."

"That's for sure," Connor added, smiling at my mother. He may even have winked at her too. "Mandy's such a good kid. If she wants a cat, why not?"

My mother laughed out loud. "I never could resist a red beard, Connor," she said. "But one accident, and it's out into the night with that cat. I don't care if the drifts are seven feet high."

"There won't be any accidents," I assured her, adding a hug for good measure.

She hugged me back and then she picked up the tray of cocoa and cookies. "If I don't get this to Carrie and Peter soon," she said, "they'll think I died. You take care of everything, Amanda Jane. I'd just as soon hear nothing more about it."

"Yes, Mother," I agreed, working hard not to sound too excited. When she was gone, I turned to Connor. "Boy," I said, "for someone who doesn't like cats, you've sure learned a lot about them."

"It's only what you told me, up in the loft that day." His voice was quiet. "Remember?"

I found that my hands were shaking. I clenched my fists. "Yes, I remember. Thank you, Connor."

He nodded slowly. "I better get going. It's almost eleven o'clock. The movie will be letting out in a couple of minutes. They always get jammed at McDonalds after the movie." But he made no motion toward leaving. He just stood there.

"You must have done some fast talking to get away at all."

"Yeah. Well."

"But you're good at that."

He smiled and reached out his hand. But then, quickly, he dropped it to his side. "Good night, Mandy," he said.

"Good night, Connor."

And then he was gone.

I decided to go down into the basement to find a box and an old blanket for Jr. to sleep in. That was her name—Trilby Jr. She had finished her milk, so I picked her up to take her with me. She was purring. I think I was purring, too.

Jr. was not the only old acquaintance to return to Winter Hill that week. Friday night, the night before the Charity Ball, the phone rang. I answered it.

"Hi." The voice on the other end sounded vaguely familiar. "Lissa?"

"No, it's Mandy. Who's this?"

"Hi, little Mandy. It's Howie Pridman. But

don't tell Lissa," he added quickly. "Just call her to the phone. I want to surprise her."

I placed the receiver down on the hall table. "Lissa," I shouted. "It's for you."

She came toward me from the kitchen, an orange in her hand. "Who is it?"

I shrugged. If Howie wanted to surprise her, why should I spoil his game?

She picked up the receiver. I plopped myself shamelessly on the bottom step and listened.

"Hello," I heard her say. "Who is this? . . . Come on, who is it? . . . Guess? . . . I don't want to guess. I don't like guessing games. Just tell me who you are." I saw the annoyance in her face; certainly Howie must have heard it in her voice. But he persisted. She looked at me and grimaced with impatience. "If you don't tell me who it is I'm going to hang up," she said. ". . . So call back, who cares? I won't answer the phone."

I didn't want her to hang up. After all, she was talking to the only guy she'd ever really liked.

"It's Howie Pridman," I whispered.

Her mouth dropped open, but she recovered quickly. "OK, Howie," she said. "That's enough . . . I was supposed to know it was you? How?

I'm not psychic. I can't recognize your voice through an imitation of Humphrey Bogart. Not even through a very bad imitation . . . No . . . No . . . No . . ." With each 'no,' her voice became more emphatic. "All right," she said finally. "If you insist. It won't do you any good." Without even saying goodbye, she hung up the phone, her lips pressed together in a tight line. "Howie's coming over," she said. "Don't you leave me. Don't you leave me for one second."

Was she still so much in love with him that she didn't trust herself alone with him? My curiosity must have shone in my eyes because she answered my unspoken questions.

"I don't trust him," she said. "He'll try something if we're alone, and I don't want to get involved with him again."

"I thought you liked him. I thought you loved him."

"What's the use of being in love with a guy who lives three thousand miles away and doesn't write letters? I've lost enough sleep over Howard Paul Pridman. I'm not losing any more."

"Boy," I said softly, "you must really like Connor if he can make you ignore Howie."

She gave me a long stare, and then she walked over and sat down next to me on the wide, curving bottom step. "What does Connor have to do with it?" she asked, frowning. "Nothing whatsoever. If I weren't going to the Charity Ball with Connor, or with anyone else, I still wouldn't go with Howie."

"That's what all those no's were for?" Howie did have a lot of nerve. Imagine thinking he could ask a girl like Lissa to the biggest dance of the year just one night before it was to take place.

She nodded. "But obviously he didn't believe them. That's why he's coming over. I'm sure, in person, between the two of us, we can convince him I meant what I said."

"I'm not saying a word," I announced quickly.

Her eyes widened. "But you'll stick with me? What kind of girl would desert her cousin in her hour of need?"

I pressed her hand. "Don't worry, I won't desert you."

"I knew you wouldn't."

"But you'll do the talking."

"Of course," Lissa agreed. "I just want a back-up. Some moral support."

"I'll nod my agreement with every phrase you utter," I assured her.

We'd hardly arranged ourselves in appropriately nonchalant positions in the back parlor when the doorbell rang. At Lissa's request, I answered it.

Howie strode into the front hall. He was taller than I had remembered, and he had grown a bushy, dark brown mustache. He had been grinning broadly as I opened the door, perfectly sure of his welcome. No one radiated self-confidence more powerfully than Howie.

But when he saw me, he stared, faintly startled, and for once there was a touch of doubt in his voice. "Mandy?"

I smiled a little. "Yes," I said. "I'm Mandy."

His eyebrows shot up. "You've changed."

"We all grow up sooner or later," I replied lightly. "Even girls like me." And then we're more mixed-up than ever, I thought to myself. Then we know why we avoided growing up for as long as we could. However, I didn't say any of that to Howie Pridman.

But Howie was done with me. "Where is she?" he asked. "Where's Miss America?"

"In the back parlor." I headed in that direction.

Howie followed. "Look, Mandy, I know you're a big reader. You must be in the middle of a book or something. Don't let me keep you."

I ignored his remark. He was behind me and couldn't see me smile. We entered the back parlor. Lissa's eyes were glued to the TV set. She barely turned her head as we came through the archway. She held on tightly to Jr., who was sitting on her lap. I always let Jr. in the back parlor or our bedrooms when we were alone in the house.

In two strides, Howie crossed the room, leaned over and kissed her. Deftly she turned her head so that his lips hit her cheek instead of her mouth. "Why so cool, Miss America?" he asked. "Aren't you glad to see me?" She had deliberately chosen not to sit on the couch. He didn't care. He perched easily on the arm of her chair.

"How are you, Howie?" she replied mildly. She turned back to the TV set. "We're watching *The Dukes of Hazzard.* Why don't you sit on the couch? You'll see better."

Howie stood up. "Sure, Miss America, if you'll sit there with me." He loped across the room, snapped off the TV set, sat down on the sofa and patted the cushion next to him. "Right here. Right where you used to be."

Lissa stared at him coldly. "Put that TV set back on, Howie. You have no right to come in here and take over. This is my house."

The roar of his laugh filled the room. "Oh, Lissa, don't you know who I am? This is Howie, your old pal, Howie. You can't fool old Howie."

"Yeah, you're a pal all right." Lissa sniffed. "Some pal. I wrote you four letters and never got one answer. Now you think you can come back into my life and disrupt it for a weekend and then walk away again. Well, you can't. So forget it. Go back to your grandmother's now and forget me. Take your cousin Didi to the dance tomorrow night."

"Didi's twelve," Howie responded drily. I tried to suppress a giggle and failed. At the sound, Howie turned suddenly to me. "You come with me, Mandy," he said. "We can double with Lissa and her date. You know I can treat a girl right. I'll pick you up in my grandfather's Mercedes. After the dance, we'll go to a nightclub in New York."

"I have a date," I replied, almost as coldly as Lissa.

"Oh." He laughed lightly. "Things have changed. I don't suppose you'd consider breaking it."

"If Lissa won't break hers, why should I?"

"Why not?" Howie grinned suggestively.

"Cut it out, Howie," Lissa complained. "You're acting like a child."

He leaned back against the sofa cushions and grinned again. "Jealous, sweetheart?" he said.

"Oh, Howie." She sighed. "Six months have gone by. I told you—everything is different."

"Really? You mean you're not impressed any longer by a Mercedes?" he joked. "That's all right. I'll hire a Rolls."

Lissa shook her head slowly. "You're incredible, Howie. Simply incredible. Not a word for half a year, and then you drop in and imagine I've been sitting in this room the whole time, my hands folded in my lap."

"Cripes, Lissa, what did you expect?" He sounded as if he were the injured party. "I'm in college now. You don't have time in college to write letters. It's not a snap like high school."

"Did you ever hear of the telephone?" she retorted. "This may come as a surprise to you, but wires do connect New Jersey and California."

"Three thousand miles is nothing to Ma Bell," I interjected.

I don't think he heard me. He stood up, crossed the room and stationed himself directly in front of her. "Oh, come on, Lissa," he said. "Break your dumb date. You know you've never really cared about any guy but me."

Deliberately, Lissa lifted Jr. from her lap and placed her on the floor. Then she stood up and faced Howie. Her reply was low and tense. "But you never really cared about me, Howie Pridman. Not for one minute. I've grown up. I don't need to like the one guy in the world who doesn't really like me. I don't need to like the one guy in the world who gives me a hard time."

That was interesting. That was very interesting. So she had been afraid. Just like me. Or so it seemed. I'd have to think more about it, later.

Howie decided to ignore the fact that I refused to leave the room. He put his arm around Lissa and before she could utter a word of protest, kissed her long and hard on the lips.

There wasn't much she could do except remain totally unresponsive. And that wasn't very much fun for Howie. He pulled away. "You're pretending, Lissa," he said. "I know when a girl's pretending." Nothing could dent his good opinion of himself. If you're tired of the adolescent identity crises of your friends, self-confidence like Howie's can be a pleasant change. But he was carrying it too far.

"Get out of here, Howie," Lissa said, her face stern, her voice low and dark. "Get out of here this minute or I'll scream."

"I'll go get Dad and Peter," I chirped helpfully. "They're only next door."

Howie stood up. "I know you're pretending, Lissa, but that's all right," he said. "You won't be able to keep it up forever." He patted the top of her head. "I'm not mad at you," he explained in a kindly tone. "I'll see you tomorrow." He smiled. "Sleep well, and dream about me." And then he strode out of the room. Neither of us moved to follow him. He let himself out.

We sat there silently, listening for the door, and when we heard it slam, we both sighed. "Did you really like him, Lissa," I queried, "or was your head turned by all that money?" Jr. was rubbing against my legs. I picked her up and stroked the back of her neck. She purred softly, letting me know I was doing exactly what she wanted.

Lissa shook her head. "What did I ever see in him? Last week I'd have told you he was the only guy I'd ever loved. Now I can't even tell you why. He kissed me, and I didn't feel a thing. How could I? He's one hundred percent obnoxious." She tossed her head so hard that her hair danced on her shoulders. It was as if she were trying to shake something out of it. Then she walked over to the TV set and snapped it on again. *The Dukes of Hazzard* had descended into its final moments of vehicular mayhem. I spoke up over the squeaks and howls of the sound track. "What did you mean when you said you've grown up and you don't have to like the one guy who doesn't like you?"

She turned down the volume and looked at me for a moment before she replied, her brow knit tight with concentration. "I guess I was just so used to having guys come after me that when Howie didn't, I was intrigued. I mean he asked me out and all of that, but you remember, he'd say he was coming over and then, half the time, he wouldn't show up. When we went to a party or out with other couples, he always paid more attention to everyone else than he did to me. He would never do what I wanted to do. I was always struggling with him. I guess that fascinated me. Well, I don't need junk like that anymore. He cured me. From now on, I like guys who like me."

"Such as Connor."

She wrinkled up her nose. "Well, Connor . . . I just don't know about Connor. He's nice.

He's fun. But I'm not in love with him or any- thing like that."

"You're not in love with anyone. You haven't been since Howie."

"And I'm certainly not in love with Howie anymore," she announced emphatically. "To- night proved that to me, for sure. I don't think I ever was in love with him. I was mystified, that's all. I was intrigued."

"And since you're not in love with anyone now and weren't in love with anyone before, you've never been in love. Not really."

There was a touch of condescension in her smile. "I'm only seventeen, Mandy. I have time."

Later, in bed, while I was waiting to warm up enough to fall asleep, I thought about that. That was one place where I was ahead of Lissa. She'd never been in love, not really. But I was in love—with Connor. Or I could be, given half a chance. There was no doubt about it. I had for- given him. How could I be mad at Jr.'s savior? Mr. Rochester had never saved anything.

Did I dream about him that night? I don't know. Perhaps. If I did, the dream was so deep I didn't remember it when I woke up in the morn- ing.

Chapter Eleven

WE MANAGED to occupy most of Saturday getting ready for the Charity Ball. It is amazing to realize that one event can stretch to fill up close to twenty-four hours. In the morning we ran downtown on last minute errands. I needed panty hose; Lissa wasn't happy with any of her thirty-two tubes of lipstick. In the afternoon, we subjected ourselves to the profound ministrations of Timothy and all his minions at the Hairafter. Following an early and extremely light supper of grilled cheese sandwiches and tea, we admired the gorgeousness of our mothers as they departed with their respective mates for a preball dinner party. This left the four bathrooms in the house entirely to us, and we managed to use up all of them, each of us soaking for half an hour in a bubble bath and investigating dehydrated make-up abandoned in various cabinets and drawers, like two little girls playing grown-up.

Then we dressed, running in and out of each other's rooms every other minute for assistance with zippers, hooks and eye shadow. And in spite of the fact that getting ready for this dance had been the sole concern of an entire day, when we heard the clang of our fortunately extremely loud doorbell ringing through the upper reaches of our house, I had to throw on my robe to run down stairs. I held Jr. in one hand as I opened the door for Connor and Rory with the other.

"Will you be ready soon?" Rory queried hopefully. "I hate being late." He was looking remarkably handsome, even for him, in a cocoa brown tuxedo with a cream-colored ruffled shirt.

"Rory," Connor assured him, "it's not necessary to be on the scene for the orchestra's first note. We can miss the whole first set, so far as I'm concerned. The disco band comes on later." Connor wouldn't waste his hard-earned cash to rent a tux. He was wearing a dark blue suit, the same one he'd worn to the wedding. But he looked much better than he had then, because of that beautiful fluffy red beard and the way, lately, he'd somehow filled out so he now appeared to be dressed in clothes that belonged to him, rather than in something out of the church rummage barrel.

"I'll hurry," I said. "I'm almost ready anyway, and so is Lissa. We just have to throw on our dresses. We'll be right down." I held the cat up for Connor to see. "But first I have to put Jr. away. Hasn't she improved since you rescued her?"

"Ten hundred percent," Connor agreed. "She's almost overweight."

I grinned and ran for the kitchen. After I'd settled Jr., I tore up the back stairs like a jack rabbit. Ten minutes later, marching behind Lissa, I paraded down again at a pace as stately as a queen's at her coronation. I took my cue from Lissa. Obviously, it will not do when your dress touches the floor to run like a hoyden. At that moment I suddenly understood how much of the historical limitation of women's activities had been reinforced by their costumes. Still, it was amusing to dress up like this—for one night.

As we entered the front parlor, Rory and Connor actually stood up. That's what I mean when I say that once in a while it's fun to dress up. Not even Rory would have stood up for us if we had been wearing blue jeans. And I wouldn't want guys to stand up for me as a rule, any more than I'd want to stand up for them every time they entered a room. For a change though, it was fun. It was like being in a play, a costume drama set . . . set when? In Regency England, or in pre-

Revolutionary Russia, or in seventeenth century France, or in any age when one could imagine glamorous women and dashing men dancing the night away in glittering ballrooms.

Then a strange thing happened. Rory's eyes went to Lissa, Connor's went to me. "How beautiful you look," they said, almost in chorus. They each took one step, Rory toward Lissa, and Connor toward me. And my heart leaped with joy.

Only to tumble back where it belonged as they both checked themselves. Rory crossed to my side and took my jacket from my hand. "What a pretty dress, Mandy," he said as he helped me into my wrap. "What a gorgeous color."

"What a pretty dress," not "What a pretty girl." But all I said as I slipped into the jacket he held for me was, "Thank you, Rory. You look wonderful."

Connor was murmuring similar, if possibly more meaningful politenesses to Lissa. Then we all went outside and climbed into Rory's car. For a few minutes we seemed to have nothing to talk about. Silence hung awkwardly in the air, like a dampening mist.

We weren't used to our clothes. We didn't recognize each other. We didn't know what to say to the elegant strangers surrounding us.

But then Connor leaned forward and put his hand on my shoulder. "Lady Amanda," he said, "may I present Lord Rory, the Duke of Ramussen? He is most anxious to make your acquaintance. I think he wishes to stand up with you for the first waltz."

I giggled. Where had Connor learned all the lingo? It did not seem likely that he was also a fan of romances by Georgette Heyer. "Thank you, Sir Connor," I simpered. "I will be most delighted if you do me the honour of introducing me to Lord Rory. And at the same time, I wish to take this opportunity to present to you my bosom bow, the Honourable Melissa Koerner."

Connor leaned back again. "Ah, Miss Koerner, delighted to make your acquaintance." He picked up Lissa's hand and kissed it. Lissa giggled too.

"My dear Lord Rory," I said, "have you nothing to say for yourself?"

"Nothing that would fit in with this conversation," Rory admitted.

"You don't like Regency England?" I asked. "Well, that's OK. We'll try something else. Tell me, Count Roroff, do you think Napoleon's troops will reach Moscow before the ball is over? Shall we ride out to see the battle in our sleighs? Won't it be the most exciting sight in the world?"

Rory didn't say anything. It was Connor who answered. "All that blood making steaming red pools in the snow. Yes, certainly the most exciting sight in the world, my dear Princess Masha."

For the rest of the ride to the country club, Connor and I kept up a similar banter, accompanied by Lissa's occasional remarks, which were never quite right, but which Connor and I generously applauded as game attempts. Rory said nothing. Every so often he just smiled a little.

A long line of cars inched up slowly to the entrance of the club. When we finally arrived beneath the portico, Connor leaped out and opened my door with a flourish. Rory also opened Lissa's door and handed her out of the car, but without any bows or arm sweeps. Chipper Gaffney took the car away. He'd been hired as a parking attendant for the evening. He was in my English class, and I wondered if it was appropriate to say hello to him. I decided it was.

We entered the clubhouse. I'd been there before, of course, millions of times. My parents belonged, and we came frequently in the summer for golf, tennis and swimming. It was no movie set country club. The walls were panelled in knotty pine and the furniture covered in faded chintz slipcovers. The house committee struggled to keep the old building in reasonable repair. A new paint job was always the item that could be postponed, always the task for which there wasn't quite enough money. It was a warm, homey, shabby old place.

But on the night of the Charity Ball it was transformed. The lights had been turned down low, and a huge fire was burning in the lobby fireplace. Next to it glowed a brilliantly decorated Christmas tree. On every side table bloomed many-blossomed red and white poinsettias in shiny brass pots. The room was jammed with men in dark tuxedos and women in brilliant jewel-colored winter gowns, removing their fur and velvet wraps as they called cheerful greetings to each other. Flushed from the cold outside, the warmth inside, the excitement of the occasion, and perhaps the liquor they had consumed at pre-ball dinner parties, their eyes and teeth seemed to sparkle like their rings and bracelets and necklaces, as if they had all put on new selves to go with their new clothes.

The club's large dining room had also undergone a magical transformation into a softly glowing ballroom. Christmas trees sparkled at either end. The bar was open and crowded already, though the guests had only just begun to trickle in from the lobby. The walls were covered with boughs of holly and pine, and the only lights were the ones over the bandstand and the candles shimmering on the little tables arranged around the edges of the room. The society band was still in the midst of the first set. Later, they would alternate with the disco band, and later still, a buffet would be served.

But in the meantime, Rory moved me out on the dance floor. His arm was firm on my back, his hand pressed mine. He knew how to dance the old dances, and he whirled me about the room with comfortable ease and a good deal of grace. We didn't talk much. I didn't mind. I was wrapped up in the music and the candlelight and the sharp sweet odor of pine. I was not at the Charity Ball with the right person, but at least I was there. I would put my mind to trying to make the right person out of Rory.

But it didn't work. Dancing with Rory wasn't bad. But when the music stopped, he was just as oblivious to the truth of me, and I was just as impatient with his conversation as we'd always been. Our relationship hadn't progressed an inch. Surely he would notice that himself pretty soon.

During a break in the music we wandered

over to the bar. Though I was under age, and Rory didn't drink, it was something to do. He ordered a Perrier with lime for himself. Of course, I wanted a Coke, but I asked for the same thing he had. If I thought that by so doing I'd save myself from a lecture, I was mistaken. We sat down at one of the little tables, and I struggled to keep my eyes open as he praised my change of libation. I had, he assured me, providentially saved myself from the loss of all my teeth by the time I was twenty-two.

Connor came to my rescue. He caught sight of us from the other side of the dance floor, and holding Lissa's arm in one hand and a beer in the other, he steered her toward our table. Under the circumstances, he couldn't manage a bow as he reached us, but he ducked his head and murmured, "My lord, my lady, may we request the inestimable privilege of joining you, or do we interrupt an intimate tête-à-tête?"

Lissa didn't wait for Connor to pull out her chair, but seated herself impatiently. "Oh, talk normally, Connor, please," she complained. "This game is making me tired. It's too much work to keep up."

"Anything you say, sweetheart," he growled. "You're the boss, sweetheart,"

"But don't be Humphrey Bogart either," she begged. "I don't like Humphrey Bogart. Howie Pridman thinks he's Humphrey Bogart."

I was the only one of the four of us seated with a clear view of the vaulted archway that led from the lobby into the ballroom. "Speak of the devil," I muttered. Three other heads swiveled in the direction I was facing. Three other pairs of eyes saw what I saw—a good-looking young man with a thick, dark brown mustache, wearing a tuxedo that fit so tightly he might just as well have been wearing bathing trunks. He was walking very slowly and very deliberately directly toward our table.

"Boy, that guy thinks he's something," Rory commented. "Who is he?"

"Howie Pridman," Connor replied.

"Lissa used to date him," I explained.

"What'd you have to say that for?" Lissa grumbled.

"I didn't know it was a secret."

She had no opportunity to utter another word. Howie had arrived. He borrowed a chair from the table next to ours and sat down between Lissa and Connor, squeezing her between Rory and himself like a slice of chicken in a sandwich. Lissa shrank toward Rory so that her shoulder was touching his, as if in an effort to remove herself as far as possible from Howie.

"Hi," Howie said. "How are you guys? Having fun?"

"It's customary to ask if you're welcome before you sit down," Lissa snapped.

"Oh, Lissa, Lissa." Howie sighed. "Have you forgotten last year's Charity Ball so soon? I never dreamed you were so fickle."

"Fickle? Me fickle?" Lissa snorted. "If that isn't the pot calling the kettle black."

"Guys are supposed to play around. Girls are supposed to be faithful." After Howie said that, he had the nerve to laugh.

Lissa merely rolled her eyes in disgust. "Where's your date anyway?" she asked.

"In your honor, Miss America, I came alone." He looked from Rory to Connor and back to Rory again. "Which one of these two amazing specimens is the lucky guy you chose?"

Connor spoke up bravely. "Lissa's with me," he said.

Howie's head turned very, very slowly toward Connor. He made no attempt to disguise the disdain in his eyes. "You? You're Lissa's date?" He uttered a short laugh and turned again to Lissa. "Is that the best you can do, Miss America? A skinny Santa Claus in a funeral director's suit?"

Words rushed out of my mouth before I realized what I was saying. It was as if Howie's remark had pulled out the stopper of a bottle in which I'd closed away great gobs of feeling. "Oh, shut up, Howie Pridman," I cried. "Connor Borne is worth ten of you. Twenty. Thirty. He looks gorgeous in his blue suit. Absolutely gorgeous. It fits him now, and it goes with his red beard."

Connor's eyes opened wide, and he stared at me. For once in his life he seemed to have nothing to say. I must have flushed as deep a red as my dress. The only thing I wanted to do was crawl under the table. But that would have done no good. There was no cloth on the table. Under it, I would have been even more absurdly visible than I already was.

Connor was not struck dumb for long. A slow grin spread over his features. "Thank you, Lady Amanda," he said. "Thank you very much."

Blushing more furiously than ever, I stared down at the tabletop and hid my hot cheeks in my hands. A warmth flooded me, and it was not merely the warmth of my embarrassment. I felt as if Connor had caressed me.

If Howie had caught our exchange, he certainly ignored it. "A Santa Claus in a funeral director's suit," he repeated. But Connor didn't really interest him very much. He quickly redirected his attention to Rory. "You look more like the princess's type," he said. "That's because you look more like me."

"Oh, Howie," Lissa interrupted impatiently, "will you just get out of here? You're annoying all of us and making a fool out of yourself."

The disco group had finished hooking into all of its equipment. They had turned out the bandstand lights in favor of a headache-inducing strobe whose whirling flashes matched the driving beat of the music they'd begun to play. Howie had to shout to be heard above the noise. "You know who you really look like in that rented tux?" he screamed at Rory. "You look like the man on top of the wedding cake. The little sugar man. I bet that's the way you make out too. Like a sugar man."

Howie seized Lissa's hand. "Let's dance, Miss America," he said.

"Cut it out," Lissa protested. She tried to pull free, but Howie tightened his grip and moved toward the floor, dragging Lissa with him. Rory knocked over his chair in his haste to reach Howie's side, the side unencumbered by Lissa. By this time, Connor and I were on our feet too. All around us couples were dancing with each other, or screaming at the top of their lungs in an effort to maintain a conversation. Between the darkness and the noise, no one else had any notion of what was going on at our table.

Rory gripped Howie's upper arm. Rory had a very large hand. Large and strong. "You let her go," Rory shouted. "Just let her go." Howie must have felt the force of Rory's grip, because he grimaced as if in pain. Almost inadvertently, he dropped Lissa's hand.

"Will you repeat that?" Rory insisted. "Outside?"

"Let's go, Sugar Man," Howie repeated cooly. "I'm not afraid of you."

Lissa, her hands now free, grabbed Rory's arm. "Rory," she cried, "don't. Don't fight him. He played football in high school."

"I play in college, too," Howie added.

"So what?" Rory shouted. Then, with wonderful gentleness, his large hand closed over Lissa's and carefully removed it from his sleeve.

I added my protests to Lissa's. "Rory, please," I said. "This is no time or place for a fight." But I sensed very clearly that if Rory wouldn't listen to Lissa, he certainly wasn't going to listen to me.

And he didn't. Perhaps he hadn't even heard me. "Coming?" he asked Howie.

Lissa changed her tactics. "Please, Howie," she said. "This is silly. People don't do things like this. Not in our day and age."

"First things first," Howie said. "I'll talk to you later, sweetheart." Rory had already started out of the room, and Howie strode jauntily after him. And then, of course, Lissa followed Howie, and, side by side, his hand tightly gripping mine, Connor and I followed Lissa. I was not so disturbed and horrified by what was going on between Rory and Howie that I was unable to enjoy the warm clasp of Connor's hand.

Outside, beyond the curving drive, a wide lawn stretched between the clubhouse and the thirteenth hole of the golf course. In the summer it was a thick green carpet; but now, in December, underneath a cold, white moon, it rolled away to the brook in a stretch of frosty, knotted brown clumps, silent and deserted. The only human being in view, besides ourselves, was Chipper Gaffney, leaning against one of the portico pillars, smoking a cigarette.

Rory and Howie squared off. Tears streamed

down Lissa's face, streaking her make-up. For the first time in all her life, she was out in public looking less than perfect. "Please, please, don't," she sobbed. "Please."

Howie ignored her. Rory glanced at her out of the corner of his eye. Connor and I stood a bit to the side, staring in total, horrified fascination. I shivered as Howie took a swipe at Rory. Connor dropped my hand and put his arm around me. Rory avoided Howie's attack with an easy, smooth, ducking motion. His fist whipped out and stung Howie on the jaw. The tightness of the grip he had experienced earlier had somehow not prepared Howie for the stunning blow, and with an automatic reflex, his hand cupped his jaw. Rory seized the opportunity to sock Howie in the stomach. Usually the soul of honor, on this occasion Rory didn't have the faintest intention of fighting fair.

With the growl of a wounded tiger, Howie slammed his hands down hard on Rory's shoulders and began to shake him. Rory grabbed one of Howie's wrists and with his huge hand squeezed until Howie was forced to let go.

And then, suddenly, with a swift, silver motion, Lissa darted between them. Once again she seized Rory's arm. She was no longer sobbing.

She was shouting, and her voice was angry. "Rory," she cried. "Rory Ramussen."

"Get out of the way, Lissa," Howie said, reaching his hands toward her.

Rory eyed Howie over Lissa's shoulder. "If you touch her," he threatened, "I'll kill you." Perhaps it was the surprising power of Rory's blows, or perhaps it was the tone of Rory's voice. Whatever it was, Howie's respect for Rory had increased about a million times in the past ten minutes. He took one step back.

Rory put his hands on Lissa's shoulders. "If you love me, Rory Ramussen," Lissa said, sounding just like a mother lecturing a disobedient child, "if you love me, you'll stop this silliness right this minute. You'll stop it right now."

"If I love you . . . if I love you," Rory murmured hoarsely, sounding more than a little bemused. Howie might just as well have been on the moon for all the notice either of them were taking of him now. "If I love you," he repeated. And then he stopped talking. He pulled her toward him and holding her tight against him, he kissed her. Her arms went around his neck, her body shaped itself to his, and they remained locked together for what seemed like half a year.

How perfectly amazing. Rory apparently

had no difficulty whatsoever in kissing a girl when he really wanted to.

I turned away. Though they were obviously totally unaware of us three spectators, I felt as if watching them were a terrible violation of their privacy. Connor lacked my delicacy. When I turned toward him, I saw that he was staring at them, a faintly amused smile lifting the corners of his mouth. "Connor," I said, "perhaps we'd better go in."

His eyes looked into mine as his lips broke into a full grin. "Yes," he agreed. "We won't be missed." He took my hand, and we started toward the club house. "Come along, Howie," Connor added in a kindly but markedly authoritative tone.

Howie seemed to have shrunk about four inches. Obediently he fell in step along side us. "Listen," he said, his face screwed up in puzzlement, "didn't you say you were Lissa's date?"

"Yes," Connor agreed, "that's what I said."

"Well, was it true?"

"Sure," Connor replied. "I wouldn't lie about a thing like that."

"Well, if that's the case, why aren't *you* out there socking the other guy in the nose? Why were you letting me do your dirty work?"

"It's funny, Howie, that you should turn out to be smarter than the rest of us," I interjected mildly. "How did you know it was Rory that Lissa really cared about?"

Howie gave Connor a poke, and Connor almost fell over. "I knew it couldn't really be this one."

I felt the blood rush to my head once more. But before I could lash out at him again, Connor's fingers were massaging my shoulder. "I'm not interested in fighting you or Rory," Connor said quietly. "That's not my line."

"You're yellow," Howie complained. "I could see that right away."

"You . . . you . . . you no good louse," I sputtered. "You shut up."

"I don't think I'm a coward," Connor replied in his customary tone of utter reasonableness. "I just think I'm sensible. You could kill me in two minutes, and Rory could kill me in one. And what reason do I have to battle either of you?"

By this time we were walking past Chipper Gaffney, still leaning against the pillar, still smoking a cigarette. He stared at the three of us as if we were as weird as a trio of Martians. But he didn't move from his post or utter a sound.

"Lissa," I said, explaining, "He thinks you should have fought him and Rory over Lissa."

"Thank you, Mandy." Connor's hand again stroked my shoulder. "I'm so glad I have you to explain things to me." I felt little shivers of sweetness run down my arm as he touched me.

Inside Howie headed for the men's room. He had some repair work to do before he could once again appear in even a dimly lit place, though what he was going to do when he came back I couldn't imagine. Maybe we'd be lucky and he'd just clean himself up and go home.

Connor and I stepped through the wide arch and into the ballroom. The strobe light was still spattering its rays on the darkness, but the disco beat had slowed. He put his arms around me, and I put mine around him. Deliberately we moved out onto the floor, the throbbing beat of the drum rising up through our feet and filling our bodies. For once, neither of us had anything to say. We just moved together with the music, as close to each other as we could get, his hand against the small of my back, caressing me as we moved, so that I felt my legs turning to delicious jelly. I closed my eyes. His lips brushed my ear, and the little shocks of pleasure that I felt at that touch made me dizzy. I could not believe what was happening to me. I could not believe I was actually dancing with Connor. I could not believe that Connor was actually holding me in his arms.

But when the music stopped, I woke up. The lights went on again over the bandstand. I stepped away from Connor, and his arms fell to his side. I felt as if someone had thrown cold water in my face. "Lissa," I whispered. "You're in love with Lissa."

He grabbed my hand. "Oh, kiddo, for a smart girl you sure are an idiot. I don't love Lissa. I never did. Not for a minute. Not for one single second."

The musicians were leaving the bandstand. The dancers had walked off the floor. Everyone was gone. Everyone except us. We stood there, in the middle of the room, holding hands, looking at each other like a pair of sheep. "You're sure?" I asked.

"Mandy, Mandy," he murmured with a sigh, "what do you think has been going on here for the last forty-five minutes? Just what do you think has been going on here?"

"I don't know, Connor. Maybe I'm fooling myself. I do that a lot."

His eyes left my face and darted around the room. "Mandy," he said, "let's get out of here. OK?"

"OK," I said.

The lobby was empty. A high-backed sofa faced the fireplace. If you scrunched down low, people walking to and from the rest rooms couldn't see you. That's what we did. We scrunched down low, and Connor kissed me, and I kissed Connor. I can't speak for Connor, but it was the first real kiss I had ever gotten, or given. As long as they live, I wish all my good friends such lovely kisses.

The rest of the evening was like a dream. Only it was more wonderful than any dream I'd ever dreamed, asleep or awake. They served a supper; I can't remember eating any of it. Somewhere in there Lissa and Rory, somewhat repaired, showed up again, and the four of us sat at a table with food in front of us, and knives and forks, but it was as if we'd forgotten what they were for. I guess we said things now and then too, and I know that we laughed a lot, but what we said or what we laughed at I have no recollection of whatsoever. The only thing I remember is Peter and Aunt Carrie and my mother and my father stopping by our table to say hello. The room was very large and crowded with half the population of Winter Hill. The younger people had congregated at one end, the older folks at the other. That's why, until then, we'd managed so successfully to avoid our parents. When I saw them approaching us, I woke up enough to pull my hand out of Connor's.

"Hi, kids," Peter said. "Having fun?"

Lissa was not as quick as I. Not until Peter spoke did she drop Rory's hand. But they had been holding hands under the table. Perhaps Peter hadn't noticed. "Oh, sure," she said, smiling up at him. "Just great."

Aunt Carrie's eyes moved quickly from one of us to the other. So did my mother's. A slight frown passed quickly over her features, and then was gone. "Well," she said, "that sure is nice."

"And you, Mother? Dad?" I queried brightly. "Are you having fun?"

"Well," my father said, "to be perfectly frank with you, I've been to enough of these affairs. I think we'll skip next year's. I think we'll go to Acapulco instead."

"Ah, Gene, you're jaded," my mother said. "To these young people the Charity Ball is still wonderful, isn't it?"

"Yes, Mother," I replied demurely. More wonderful than you know, I thought to myself. Crazy, but wonderful.

Soon after, we left. Only this time, Lissa sat in the front of the car with Rory, and I sat in the back with Connor. I was the lucky one. Connor wasn't driving, which left him free to do other things.

At an all-night diner out on the highway we ate doughnuts and toasted muffins and drank coffee. A huge, ugly clock on the wall behind the counter read twenty minutes after two. Lissa stared at it, and it stared back at her unblinkingly. "We have to go home," she said with a sigh. "They'll be wondering what happened to us." We had no specific curfew, but we were expected to be in at what was termed "a reasonable hour," and we had always sensed that the freedom we enjoyed depended upon our not betraying expectations founded upon trust.

I leaned my head against the back of the booth and shut my eyes. I was tired—exhausted, really. "So much has happened tonight," I said, "it'll take me three or four months to straighten it all out in my head."

"It's quite simple, really," Connor said. "You were right from the beginning. Lissa and Rory were made for each other. They liked each other all along."

I opened my eyes with a jerk and leaned forward across the table. "Lissa," I accused, "is that the truth?"

But I knew the answer to my question was yes. "So why all that pretended indifference?" I cried. "Why all those secret arrangements to fix me up with Rory? You caused yourself so much misery, and you made me so mad."

"Me?" Lissa protested, her voice pained. "Me? What about you? Interfering in everyone's lives and botching it all up."

"That's right, Lissa," Connor agreed with a laugh, "you tell her. Give it to her good."

"You were no help either, Connor," I retorted, squeezing his hand hard. But he only squeezed mine right back. He was no Howie Pridman, but he could still squeeze a lot harder than I could. "Listen, Lissa," I went on, "is that why you pretended you didn't care for Rory? Just because you were annoyed at me for trying to get the two of you together."

"Of course not," Lissa groaned. "I don't usually bite off my nose to spite my face." She struggled to find the words with which to explain herself. "I was afraid of liking Rory. You know, the only other guy I'd ever really cared about was Howie Pridman, and he was terrible to me. I guess I thought a girl was a lot better off going out with a guy she didn't really like too much. And you know the other thing. I didn't want to make it so easy for Peter and Mother. And then when I realized that you liked Rory . . ." Her voice trailed off.

"You did, you know," Connor accused me. "Admit it, you did."

"*I* thought so," Rory interjected mildly.

I turned on him like an avenging fury. "But you didn't like me. It was Lissa you wanted all along. You never even kissed me. You kissed Lissa fast enough when you had the chance."

Connor's eyebrows shot up. "What's the matter, kiddo? You're not jealous, are you?" Beneath his bushy red brows, his eyes were full of mischief.

I leaned back in my seat. "No, of course not. Just curious, that's all. I don't understand."

"That's your trouble, Mandy," Lissa said in a kindly tone. "You have to know the reasons for everything. For you there can never be any mysteries."

I had always thought she was the literal one and I was the one deviled by imagination, but I wasn't going to argue with her. "Explain anyway," I said. "You explain, Rory." At the moment he seemed the most rational one in the crowd.

"If Lissa was afraid of me, can you imagine

how afraid I was of her?" Rory admitted candidly. "I just kept telling myself she was my sister, she was my sister. I didn't admit to myself how crazy I was about her until I saw that hulk lay his hands on her."

"Of course, her going out with me didn't bother you at all," Connor said. It was his turn now to sound a little miffed.

"Rory knew there was nothing between you and me except a few laughs," Lissa said. "For me, it was a pleasant relief." Her eyes caught Connor's for a moment. "If you'll excuse me for saying so," she added apologetically.

Connor decided to be gracious. "That's all right, Lissa. I understand. Believe me, I enjoyed it. It was a new thing for me, going out with the most popular girl in Winter Hill. I got a kick out of it, and it certainly didn't hurt my reputation any."

"What's going to happen to your reputation now?" I asked.

He grinned. "It can look after itself."

I turned to Rory once again. "I still don't know why you pretended to be interested in me."

"I wasn't pretending," he protested. "I like you. You're a nice girl. You're smart, and you're a good listener." He still had no idea of who I really was. "I've never dated much," he admitted softly. "I've kind of stayed away from girls. I guess I just really didn't trust them."

So you decided to start on an easy, harmless one, I thought to myself. But that was OK. No problems, no pressure, like Lissa and Connor. But there were going to be problems now, there was going to be pressure now, for all four of us. Well, we'd work it all out. It was a very good thing that Lissa and I had parents who did have certain expectations concerning us. That Lissa and I had certain expectations concerning ourselves was even more to the point.

I faced Connor. "You see?" I said. "I was right. I was right from the beginning. Both Lissa and Rory mistrust all those kids who come running after them. They wanted someone who sees beyond their beautiful faces. They wanted each other."

"But you do understand what happened, don't you, Mandy?" Lissa said earnestly. "Once I realized that you liked Rory, and once I saw him taking an interest in you, I had to lay low. You were my friend. You were the only one who had understood what I went through at the time of the wedding."

"I understood," Rory said.

She smiled at him. Dazzled, he blinked his eyes. "Yes, Rory," she said. "I know you did."

"There's a lot I still don't understand," I complained.

"Oh, Mandy!" Lissa exclaimed. "So what? The important thing is that it all got sorted out. It all got sorted out before it was too late."

Connor was still grinning. He had been more or less grinning steadily since we had walked back into the clubhouse after the fight—except when we were kissing. "And to think," he said, "that we owe it all to Howie Pridman."

It was a delicious conversation. I could have pursued it until dawn. But Lissa was right. The evening had to end. There would be other nights, and other days.

Chapter Twelve

THE PORCH LIGHT was on when we got home. The house was waiting for us. The kisses we exchanged before going inside were chaste little pecks. The house was somehow inhibiting. I felt as if it were watching us.

Which, in a way, it was. For when we got inside, we found a reception committee. The light was on in the front parlor. As soon as the door closed behind us, Aunt Carrie's voice called out, "Lissa, that you?"

"Yes, Mom, it's me," Lissa called back.

"It's me too, Aunt Carrie," I chimed in.

"Come in here, please, both of you," Aunt Carrie invited.

We obeyed. Mother and Aunt Carrie, in their bathrobes, were sitting on the sofa in front of the double windows, a pot and cups on the coffee table in front of them.

"Would you care for some tea?" my mother asked, as if it were three o'clock in the afternoon instead of three o'clock in the morning.

"No thanks," I said. "We just had a bite at the diner. I'm tired. I think I'll go to bed."

"Please sit down, Amanda Jane," my mother said. Her voice was mild, but I knew an order when I heard it. I sat down.

"You too, Lissa," Aunt Carrie added.

Lissa also sat down. "I know it's late," she apologized. "But not too late. Not too late for the Charity Ball. It wasn't exactly a normal night."

"No, it certainly wasn't," my mother agreed. "You'll pardon our natural curiosity, but what's going on?" She didn't sound angry, exactly, but there was an odd quality to her voice. I wondered what we had done wrong. Perhaps we *had* come in too late. Perhaps the tacit understanding between us did not stretch to three a.m., not even on the night of the Charity Ball.

But suddenly a note of unaccustomed hesitation crept into her voice. She actually sounded more than a little uncomfortable. "You see . . . we were . . . well, Carrie and I . . . we were sort of watching you."

I did not let the opportunity to seize the initiative pass. "Watching us? What do you mean, watching us? Do you mean spying?"

"I guess you could call it that," Aunt Carrie

admitted, rather sheepishly. "When we heard you on the porch we opened the drape just a crack and peeked out."

No wonder I'd felt the house had eyes. It did.

"Really, Mother," Lissa said coldly, "it's hard for me to imagine your doing such a thing. You're supposed to trust me, and I'm supposed to be worthy of your trust. That's always been our method, and it's worked so far. I don't think you can object to a kiss. I am seventeen, you know."

"Oh, Lissa," Aunt Carrie said with a slight, embarrassed giggle, "I didn't think you were doing anything wrong. The only thing is, at the ball we couldn't help noticing that you danced more with Rory than you did with Connor . . ."

"And," my mother interjected, turning to me, "you danced more with Connor than you did with Rory."

How dense of me to have imagined them too busy with their own good time to notice us! It really was incredible that the Charity Ball had survived in its traditional form for so many decades. Hanging out at opposite ends of the room doesn't save a person from the x-ray vision of parents, or at least of our parents.

"And then," Aunt Carrie added, "when we

heard you on the porch, we couldn't help peeking. Connor kissed you, Mandy, and Rory kissed Lissa. Mandy left with Rory and came home with Connor. Lissa left with Connor and came home with Rory. Will someone please tell us what's going on?"

Lissa and I glanced at each other. I pressed my lips together, but laughter dribbled out between them anyway. Lissa smiled and shook her head. Truly, how could we explain?

"I don't see what's so funny, Amanda Jane," my mother said. She sounded hurt.

"Oh, Mother," I cried, "it's so complicated, explanations would take hours. And all the explanations in the world won't make it sound reasonable."

"I really liked Rory all along, and Mandy really liked Connor," Lissa said soothingly. "Do you understand now?"

"Certainly not," Aunt Carrie retorted.

"If that's the case, why was Rory dating Mandy and Connor dating you?" my mother asked me with indisuptable logic.

"Because we got all mixed up!" I exclaimed impatiently. "No one knew how anyone else really felt. Actually, no one knew how they felt themselves."

"But we got it all sorted out tonight," Lissa said. "Thank goodness."

"Thank Howie Pridman," I interjected.

Aunt Carrie and my mother looked more mystified than ever. Who could blame them? "We'll explain it in the morning," I said. "Maybe when we're not so tired, we can all make more sense out of it."

Mother pushed her teacup toward the pot. "We'd better let them go to bed, Caroline," she said.

"I doubt we'll ever get to the bottom of it, Mary Belle," Aunt Carrie replied as she rose from the sofa. "Let's leave the tea things until morning."

My mother got up, too. "Well, good night, girls," she said. "At least you all appeared to have a good time. I'm glad of that, anyway.

"Did you?" I remembered to ask. "Daddy was a little bored."

She looked somewhat startled at my question. "Oh, but we had a nice time. Of course we did. A very nice time." Then she looked at Aunt Carrie. Some sort of message passed between them, and their eyes crinkled in little smiles. They left the parlor together and climbed up the stairs.

"It's nice how they've always had each

other," I said. They quarreled sometimes, especially in the kitchen, but they were also each other's best friend.

"Like us," Lissa said.

I nodded slowly. "That's right," I agreed. "But we didn't know that until recently." I rose, reached out my hand and pulled her out of her seat. And then we two followed our mothers up the stairs.

The next morning, when Connor called before he went to work, I remembered something. "Connor," I said, "the bet. I won the bet."

"No, you didn't," Connor said. "The bet was that Rory would take Lissa to the Charity Ball. He didn't take her. I took her."

"He took her home," I retorted. "That's what matters."

"It may be what matters," Connor replied, "but the bet didn't say anything about that."

"You're a cheat, Connor. I always knew it."

"Let's call it a draw," he suggested. "That's fair."

"OK," I agreed. "So now I want to know what you didn't win and what I didn't win."

"Isn't it a good thing I didn't let you look in the envelope last week, when you were so sure that I'd won?" Connor gloated. "Isn't it?"

"Well, now I want to know. Tell me."

But he wouldn't. No matter how much I begged him, he wouldn't. He said the next day we'd get the envelope from Miss Dreyfuss and look inside. There was just a faint trace of discomfort in his voice as he put me off, and after a while I caught it and stopped pressing him.

Monday, during lunch, we found Miss Dreyfuss at her desk in the publications room. Connor asked her for the envelope he'd sent her to hold for him, and she pulled it out of her drawer. "You're a little crazy, Connor," she said. "Do you know that?"

"Oh, no crazier than anyone else, Miss Dreyfuss," he said. He meant, "No crazier than you, Miss Dreyfuss."

She waved the envelope under his nose. "Will you please tell me what this is all about?"

Connor laughed. Once again, that faint trace of discomfort was audible in his tone. "Maybe someday, Miss Dreyfuss. Not now."

She withdrew her hand. "Well, then, maybe I just won't give you this envelope."

"Why, Miss Dreyfuss," Connor said lightly, "I never knew you to be such a tease. Now what do you want me to do to get that envelope?"

Miss Dreyfuss smiled and tossed her head so that her tight gray curls bounced around like tiny

hot dogs. I realized with a shock that Miss Dreyfuss had a crush on Connor. I wondered that I
had never noticed that before. Well, for most of
my life I'd never thought of Connor as someone
people had crushes on. And more recently, I had
been too preoccupied with my own crush and
what I thought was Lissa's to notice anyone
else's.

"Promise me you'll meet the next yearbook
deadline even if you and I have to stay here until
midnight," Miss Dreyfuss said.

"Oh, I promise, I promise," Connor agreed.

"Even if they offer you thirty dollars an hour
at McDonalds," she added.

"You come first, Miss Dreyfuss," he assured
her. He knew just how to handle her.

She smiled again and dropped the envelope
into his outstretched hand. "Thank you, Miss
Dreyfuss," he said.

"You're welcome, Connor," she replied.
Then she shot me a knowing little glance from
under her lashes. I wondered if she had steamed
open the envelope and then resealed it. That
would have been a suitably Victorian thing for
Miss Dreyfuss to do.

But Connor was done with Miss Dreyfuss.
He grabbed my hand and we went out into the

hall. He handed me the envelope without saying a word.

I checked the postmark. It was dated October 19, two days after Carrie's and Peter's wedding. Then I tore open the tightly sealed flap, pulled out the sheet of paper inside, unfolded it and read the words that were neatly typewritten on the white page.

IF RORY TAKES LISSA TO THE CHARITY BALL, CONNOR MUST DELIVER TO MANDY EXACTLY AT MIDNIGHT ON NEW YEAR'S EVE TEN KISSES. IF RORY DOES NOT TAKE LISSA TO THE CHARITY BALL, MANDY MUST DELIVER SAME TO CONNOR.

I laughed so loud when I read those words that all the way down at the other end of the corridor, kids turned and stared at me, and then they smiled too, even though they had no idea what was so funny. "You've got nerve, Connor," I said. "How did you know I'd want to?"

"I didn't," Connor said. "I was just hoping."

I took his hand. "Connor, it was me," I said softly. "It was me all along."

He nodded.

"Why didn't you say something?" I asked. "Why didn't you do something?"

"You were oblivious to me," he replied quietly.

"You were always my friend," I said.

"You know what I mean. I knew I was kind of funny-looking."

"You!" I exclaimed. "You? What about me?"

"I always thought you were adorable."

"Even before the hair cut and the clothes?"

He nodded. "What do they have to do with anything, really?"

"Oh, Connor," I moaned, "we wasted so much time."

"Not really," he said. "You weren't ready, and neither was I. I didn't have the confidence to make a move. Lissa helped me get over that."

"I guess Rory helped me too, then," I admitted. "Maybe it's good to practice on someone you don't care about too much."

Connor pointed to the piece of paper I still held in my hand. "I was able to write down a wish that I never could have expressed out loud," he said. "But boy, did it gripe me the day of the wedding when you set up your whole crazy scheme. As long as there was no one else, I didn't feel too bad. But when I thought you really liked Rory. . . ." He shook his head, and for a moment his face was covered with remembered gloom.

"So I just nodded and sort of went along with Lissa when she made her plans. Actually I tried not to do too much of anything, one way or the other. Because I really wanted you, Mandy. All along. Even when I was mad at you."

I wished I could have said that I'd known all along that Connor was the one, as he had known that I was, but that would have been a lie. And anyway, he had recognized my crush on Rory. I couldn't lie to Connor, at least not now. "I was mad at you too," I said. "But then I couldn't stay mad."

He laughed a little. "We didn't get very far with *Much Ado About Nothing*. We did much better with *All's Well That Ends Well*."

There was a rule that said the most a girl and boy could do in the school building was hold hands. I mean they actually had such a rule. It was not one of the rules the teachers took much delight in enforcing, and it was broken with great regularity. It had always disgusted me, the sight of couples making out against the lockers. I didn't plan to join that crowd. Not that I objected to what they were doing so much as I did to where they were doing it. Some things are private, that's all.

But at that moment I had to do what I felt

like doing. I stood up on my tiptoes and gave Connor a quick, light kiss on his ear.

Connor smiled. "Thank you, Mandy," he said. And then he took my hand. We walked slowly down the long, dim, briefly silent corridor. Maybe we ate lunch that day, and maybe we didn't. I can't remember. But I can remember Connor and his red beard and his hand holding mine. I'll remember that forever.

Two Hearts

...Because when you read about love, you're ready for it

---

*We can't promise you a date on Saturday night, but we can
promise you a good time when you curl up with a
Two Hearts™ romance!*

IN THE MIDDLE OF A RAINBOW by Barbara Girion
(21080-6)
When a chance meeting brings handsome Todd Marcus into
her life, Corrie finds herself believing that dreams can come
true!

LOVER'S GAMES by Barbara Cohen
(21081-4)
When Mandy attempts to fix up her cousin Lissa with
Lissa's gorgeous new stepbrother, her matchmaking results
in a comedy of errors!

ROADSIDE VALENTINE by C.S. Adler
(21146-2)
Seventeen-year-old Jamie is not about to let anyone stand in
the way of his love for Louisa—not even Louisa's
boyfriend!

VACATION FEVER! by Wendy Andrews
(21083-0)
Temperatures are on the rise and romance is in the air when
Mia meets a handsome stranger on a family vacation!

$2.25 each

Pacer

BOOKS FOR YOUNG ADULTS

Available at your local bookstore or library.

Join in the fun when
THE ZODIAC CLUB™ meets
again in the following books:

THE STARS UNITE
(21106-3)

When summer doldrums hit, Abby Martin and her friends decide to change their fortunes by forming a club based on Abby's new passion, astrology. Little do they realize what the stars hold in store!

ARIES RISING
(21107-1)

What could be more perfect for Abby, an Aries, than a bike trip to Ram's Head Mountain at the spring equinox? Joining her science class on the trip means passing up a Zodiac Club weekend party, but Abby is ready for some adventure of her own...

TAURUS TROUBLE
(21109-8)

When Danny Burns scoops Cathy Rosen's story during their internship at the local newspaper, Cathy, a Leo, is roaring mad. Can she grab the bull by the horns and put the arrogant Taurus in his place?

LIBRA'S DILEMMA
(21108-X)

When Mara's boyfriend, Doug, is involved in a cheating scandal at Collingwood High, it's hard for Mara, the perfect Libra, to remain an impartial judge. Should she defend the guy she loves—or the principles she lives by?

$1.95 each